DEDICATION

To all my lions out there.
It's never easy to fight and stand up for what you
believe in,
but it's a thousand times harder
to look inward and face your demons.

"Hey." Charge reached out and took her hand, giving it a squeeze. "It'll get easier. I promise."

The warmth of his touch soothed her nerves. After a lifetime of being set aside, his belief in her was everything.

She looked up, locking eyes with him. Several moments passed, the two staring at each other, while her pulse revved. Charge was so nerve-racking, but at the same time, she'd never met anyone like him. Masculine. Sure. Mesmerizing.

"Don't," he said.

"What?"

"You know what."

Crap, I was just getting all doe-eyed over him. She looked away, feeling her cheeks flush.

"It's not that you're not…" He cleared his throat. "There are rules. Operators cannot fraternize. It's a distraction, and distractions cost lives."

"Sure. Of course." She felt mortified that he'd even picked up on her thoughts. Not that she really wanted him. It was more of an admiration situation.

"Good. Glad you understand. Because there is nothing more important than protecting the team, and you won't be able to do that if you're busy playing favorites." He got back into his car. "Be careful tonight." He shut the door and drove off.

Emily sighed with a heavy feeling in her chest. Charge had just pushed her out of the nest, and whether he admitted it or not, tonight was definitely a test.

Would she pass or die?

OTHER WORKS BY
M.O. MACK

SUITE #45 SERIES
(Chick Thriller/Suspense/Action)
She's Got the Guns (Book 1) ← You should go here. Chick Thriller!
She's Got the Money (Book 2) ← You are here. ☺

ROMANCES BY MIMI JEAN PAMFILOFF

COMING SOON!
Vampire Man (The Librarian's Vampire Assistant, Book 6)
Lord King (The King Series, Book 7)
Baby, Please (OHellNo, #7) ← Yummy football player with a baby, anyone?
God of Temptation (The Immortal Matchmakers, FINALE)

THE ACCIDENTALLY YOURS SERIES
(Paranormal Romance/Humor)
Accidentally in Love with…a God? (Book 1)
Accidentally Married to…a Vampire? (Book 2)
Sun God Seeks…Surrogate? (Book 3)
Accidentally…Evil? (Novella, Book 3.5)
Vampires Need Not…Apply? (Book 4)
Accidentally…Cimil? (Novella, Book 4.5)
Accidentally…Over? (FINALE, Book 5)

THE BOYFRIEND COLLECTOR DUET
(New Adult/Suspense)
The Boyfriend Collector, Part 1
The Boyfriend Collector, Part 2

FANGED LOVE
(Standalone/Paranormal/Humor)

THE FATE BOOK DUET
(New Adult/Humor)
Fate Book
Fate Book Two

THE FUGLY DUET
(Contemporary Romance)
fugly
it's a fugly life

THE HAPPY PANTS SERIES
(Standalones/Romantic Comedy)
The Happy Pants Café (Prequel)
Tailored for Trouble (Book 1)
Leather Pants (Book 2)
Skinny Pants (Book 3)

IMMORTAL MATCHMAKERS, INC., SERIES
(Standalones/Paranormal/Humor)
The Immortal Matchmakers (Book 1)
Tommaso (Book 2)
God of Wine (Book 3)
The Goddess of Forgetfulness (Book 4)
Colel (Book 5)
Brutus (Book 6)
God of Temptation (FINALE) ← 2021!

THE KING SERIES
(Dark Fantasy/Suspense)
King's (Book 1)
King for a Day (Book 2)
King of Me (Book 3)
Mack (Book 4)
Ten Club (Book 5)

The Dead King (Book 6)
Lord King (Book 7) Coming 2021

THE LIBRARIAN'S VAMPIRE ASSISTANT
(Standalones/Mystery/Humor)
The Librarian's Vampire Assistant (Book 1)
The Librarian's Vampire Assistant (Book 2)
The Librarian's Vampire Assistant (Book 3)
The Librarian's Vampire Assistant (Book 4)
The Librarian's Vampire Assistant (Book 5)
Vampire Man (Book 6) Coming May 4th, 2021

THE MERMEN TRILOGY
(Dark Fantasy/Suspense)
Mermen (Part 1)
MerMadmen (Part 2)
MerCiless (Part 3)

MR. ROOK'S ISLAND TRILOGY
(Contemporary/Suspense)
Mr. Rook (Part 1)
Pawn (Part 2)
Check (Part 3)

THE OHELLNO SERIES
(Standalones/New Adult/Romantic Comedy)
Smart Tass (Book 1)
Oh Henry (Book 2)
Digging A Hole (Book 3)
Battle of the Bulge (Book 4)
My Pen is Huge (Book 5)
Wine Hard, Baby (Book 6)
Baby, Please (Book 7) ← COMING SOON!

WISH, a Standalone Novel
(Romantic Comedy)

SHE'S GOT THE MONEY

A suite #45 novel

Book Two

M.O. MACK

Copyright © 2021 by M.O. Mack
Print Edition

All rights reserved. No part of this publication may be reproduced, distributed, or transmitted in any form or by any means, including photocopying, recording, or other electronic or mechanical methods, without the prior written permission of the writer, except in the case of brief quotations embodied in critical reviews and certain other noncommercial uses permitted by copyright law.

This is a work of fiction. Names, characters, places, brands, media, and incidents are either the product of the author's imagination or are used fictitiously. The author acknowledges the trademarked status and trademark owners of various products referenced in this work of fiction, which have been used without permission. The publication/use of these trademarks are not authorized, associated with, or sponsored by the trademark owners.

Cover Design: Earthly Charms
Developmental Editing: Stephanie Elliot
Copyediting and Proof Reading: Pauline Nolet
Formatting: Paul Salvette

SHE'S
GOT THE
MONEY

CHAPTER ONE

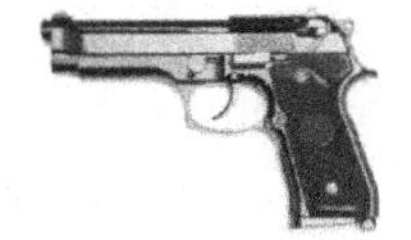

Emily Wilson stood with her feet apart, a big-ass gun in her hand, wondering if she was in over her head. Of course she was. Otherwise, she wouldn't be here.

"So I squeeze the trigger like this?" She extended her arms, pointing the weapon at the target—three empty beer cans perched atop a rotting log about fifty yards away.

Charge crossed his arms over his wide chest and gave her a nod. He was the very definition of unreadable, but today, the icy hit man was all sorts of emotion. Predatory gleams and twitching pale gray eyes, like a hungry wolf about to tear apart its prey. Was he regretting his choice to train her or simply frustrated by her lack of progress?

If he'd stop staring like that, I could focus. It would also help if he didn't dress like that.

Charge, who was in his early thirties, had thick black hair and a scruffy short beard. He was all ruggedness and jagged edges, right down to his gruff voice. He favored snug T-shirts, jeans, and baseball caps over the fine Italian suits hit men wore in movies.

Very bad. The problem being that while Charge thought he looked like a muscled badass, never to be challenged unless you wanted your entire arm shoved up your ass, she found his body to be a huge distraction.

Not that Charge was the type any sane woman would get involved with. He was fearless, in control of his emotions, entirely pragmatic, and deadly as fuck. Not dating material. Not relationship, husband, or anything-kind material. Simply put, he killed people for a living.

"What are you waiting for?" he grumbled, unhooking his mirrored sunglasses from the neck of his white T-shirt and sliding them on.

Thank God. No more eye contact. "Sorry. Just doing a little visualization first—like you taught me." The sun was just coming up behind her, and with it would come the El Paso summer heat. For the moment, it helped her see her target more clearly.

Emily relaxed her shoulders and tightened her grip on the gun, resting the butt squarely in her left palm. *Just breathe. Just breathe. You can hit it.* If she didn't, Charge would make her stand out here in the middle of nowhere until the sun went down, just like he'd done the last two days. He believed that suffering was the best teacher.

Just hit the target. Just—

She squeezed, and the gun went off like a cannon, recoiling toward her face.

"Next time keep your eyes open," Charge grumbled, his voice sounding like a bear that hadn't been fed in months.

She opened one eye to inspect her handiwork. The cans were in the dirt. "Yes!" She pointed with her left hand. "I hit 'em!" It was the first time—a big accomplishment for a woman who hated guns.

She did a little clogging dance in the dirt with her chunky military boots.

Charge shook his head disapprovingly.

"Sorry." Emily's stomach roiled. She knew the clock was ticking. Once her training was over, Charge would be gone. For good. No one could be a hit man, let alone manage an entire group of them, while being hunted by every bad guy south of the border.

He'd recently blown his cover after one of his operators went missing. Charge did everything to get the man back, including showing photos around town, but it had been a waste. They'd chopped the poor guy to pieces. And now everyone knew who Charge was.

That was where she came in. A nobody. No

education. No job experience. All she had was her determination to survive. It was her drive that got her away from Ed, her late husband, who'd been a corrupt FBI agent. That same drive had stopped him from trafficking women. Now, she was determined to never live in fear again. Every punch, every black eye, every slap Ed had given her would be her fuel.

Fucking Ed. Asshole. Scum. And a dead man, thanks to Charge, the reason she was here. She'd had nothing when she showed up in El Paso and landed a job with him, answering the phone for his "pest control" company—a cover for his real business: killing. Then he and his team took out Ed and his depraved little crew, including Ed's brother, Merrill. The women Ed and his buddies had been trafficking were freed.

Of course, there'd been one tiny hiccup. Wasn't there always? Charge's team expected her to pay them a one-million-dollar fee, but for reasons beyond her control, the operators of suite forty-five—aka Charge's team—never got their money. Mostly because the funds were supposed to come from Ed's stash, and he died before he could be persuaded to divulge the whereabouts of his piggy bank.

No money meant a group of very unhappy hit men.

And right there, *that* had sealed the deal. She could either join them and work off her debt or be put out to pasture. *Or run.* Strange to think of her coworkers as her potential executioners. But maybe working for them would make her immune to fear.

First things first, learn how to really use a gun. "I'll go reset the cans and try again. Eyes open this time." She started the march toward the log.

"I think that's all for today."

She stopped and turned. Charge held out his large, calloused hand for the gun.

"But don't you want me to—"

"I have business to take care of, and you have a new office to set up."

She raised her arm over her face to block the sun glaring in her eyes. "But I only hit the target once. Are you sure you don't want me to shoot a few more rounds?"

His hand remained open and waiting. His light gray eyes gave nothing away about this change of plans. She hoped he wasn't just coming up with an excuse to leave because he'd had it with her, but if she'd learned one thing about Charge, he didn't debate. He didn't negotiate. *Whatever he says goes.*

Like a good student, she switched on the safety and gave over the weapon. "I guess I could use a day to work on the new office." The last one had been blown up. By Charge, actually. He'd wanted to erase his footsteps as well as teach her a lesson: Be ready to set up shop elsewhere at the drop of a hat because you never knew when your cover would be blown. The work this team did was way too important to be stalled or delayed. They killed people, bad people.

Okay, yes. And they also made a shitload of cash while doing it. But what could she say? There were the Eds of the world, who exploited innocent women for money, and then there were these guys. They exploited their own talents for money.

"So tomorrow, then?" she said, pushing her shaggy locks from her brow. It was probably time for a haircut and touch-up on her red roots. Maybe that's what she'd do with her extra time today. Buy some scissors and more chestnut brown number seven—part of her new Emily Wilson identity. Brunette. Brown eyes. Twenty-six. Five-five. Really she had red hair, green eyes and was twenty-five years old. The height matched.

"I'm busy tomorrow." He started walking toward his car of the week—a black GT Charger. The irony of his muscle car wasn't lost on her.

She followed, since he was her ride. She didn't own a car. In fact, at the moment, she was sleeping on a cot in the old bookstore-slash-coffee shop they'd leased for their new office. The plan was to turn it into a private art gallery. Appointment only. It would be the perfect cover for the suite forty-five crew since it wasn't open to the public. It also had a walk-in safe in the back since the building had originally belonged to a local credit union.

Emily slid into the black leather passenger seat, waiting for Charge, who was storing the guns and ammo in the trunk.

It was strange. Now that she'd decided to take his place as manager of the group—totally insane, but it was at his insistence, not hers—her perspective of the world was changing. The old her would have never dreamed of picking up a gun or fighting anyone. Mostly because she had no muscles to speak of on her overly slender frame, and she possessed zero fighting skills. She'd always been too afraid of what would happen if she fought back. Ed had taught her that. *"The nail gets the hammer."* You stick out, you make waves, you draw attention or ruffle feathers, and you'd better be ready to get your ass kicked. Ed had been a fucking animal. She almost wished he was alive and in prison instead. Death was too good for a man like him.

"You okay?" Charge now sat behind the wheel, staring down with that intense look in his eyes.

Emily snapped out of her dark thoughts. "Yeah. Sorry. Did you say something?"

"I'll be gone for a few days. I'd like you to train with Flint and Olivia while I'm away."

"Who are they?"

"Operators fifteen and seven."

Each operator was assigned a number. Charge was number forty-five. That was actually how their group's name originated. Forty-five people. A team with one common goal: killing criminals. Sadly, they were down to thirty-eight operators now. Seven open slots. Sooner or later, they'd have to start bringing in new operators— something she wasn't sure how to do. She didn't even know how to get hold of the team, where to procure weapons and supplies, how clients hired them, or how all the money flowed. Charge didn't feel it was time yet to disclose such sensitive information. *"Prove yourself first; then you get the keys to Sampson."*

Sampson was the group's official leader, his true identity never revealed to the team or anyone. Well, except to her, of course. Sampson was actually a title, a role, responsible for vetting every job. Sampson also handled the money, kept an eye out for the team, and ensured they had what they needed to carry out jobs. There'd been quite a few Sampsons over the years from what she gathered, Charge being the most recent. To the crew, however, Charge was simply operator forty-five. They had no idea he was the boss.

Like Charlie from Charlie's Angels. Soon, she would be the new Sampson, the manager, but that meant she had to pretend to become part of the crew, too. To sell that story, she had to at least know how to fire a weapon like a pro so she could go on a few team jobs.

Her stomach lurched. The thought of carrying out a hit didn't sit well, but the day was fast approaching, and she knew it.

What am I going to do? Managing them was one thing, but actually being a hit man was another. She just didn't have it in her.

CHAPTER TWO

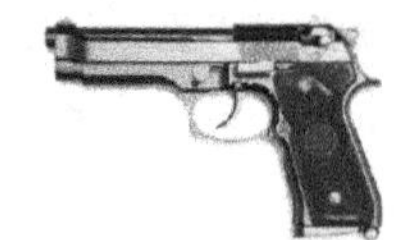

After a short drive filled with awkward silence, Charge and Emily pulled up in front of the old bookstore. The Spanish-style building, with its arched windows and a red tile roof, was located in a quiet upscale part of town filled with cute little bistros and boutiques. Just the place no one would think to look for their office.

"I will ask you one more time. What's the matter? You look green." Charge put his car in park, his deep voice sounding displeased. What was new?

"Nothing. I've just been thinking."

"Want my advice?"

"Sure." She nodded.

"Don't."

"Don't what?"

"Think. When the time comes, you learn the protocols. You follow them. You do your job.

That's it."

She scoffed. "Are you trying to tell me you never stop to really consider the impact of taking lives?"

"No."

"But you've gotta feel something about what you do."

"How many people in this world have casual sex—maybe one too many drinks before a Saturday night hookup, which ends up in making a life? You think those people are giving thought to the magnitude of their decisions while they're fucking in the back seat of a Chevy?"

"Well, some yes. Some no."

"Exactly. I am a 'some no.'"

She shook her head and exhaled slowly. They were so different. Yet, at the same time, she admired Charge. He was everything brave in this world. He didn't hesitate to put his life on the line for what he believed in. She, on the other hand, didn't even know who she was.

She knew who she used to be: Ed's punching bag.

She knew how she wanted to feel: Never afraid again.

She knew what she was capable of: Bravery when it came to helping others.

But *who* was she? Justine Hays was the name on her birth certificate from Maine, her home state. But Justine was the woman who used to belong to Ed. She was also the daughter of the dearly departed Big Carl and Aunt Mary, who was a mother to her after her own mom took off. Justine dreamed of becoming a veterinarian and filling her house with the sorts of pets no one would adopt—the one-eyed cats and three-legged dogs of the world. She wanted to find love, get married, maybe have a human family someday.

Then there was Emily Rockford, the first fake identity, but that cover had been blown. She'd been a woman on the run, surviving day to day.

Finally, there was Emily Wilson. She was a fresh blank page. *Emily Wilson has extreme baggage she needs to dump.*

Emily stared into Charge's cool gray eyes. "I'm just not sure I'll ever think of this job as something casual, like you do."

"I never said that. I simply meant that some of us don't fixate on what needs to be done. I remove predators from the world. I get paid for it. Not much to think about."

"Okay, but..." Her voice trailed off. She wanted to talk about what had happened to her at that bus terminal in Denver after she'd refused Charge's initial offer to train her and put her at the helm. He claimed her scrappiness was just what the team needed. Also, she could easily fly under the radar. A woman like her—young, no weapons training, no formal leadership skills— wasn't your typical ringleader. But it hadn't been

Charge's beliefs that convinced her to return to El Paso and accept the job. It was the fact that while she was leaving town, she'd killed someone at that bus terminal, and it gave her a glimpse of a different version of herself. A lion. Not a lamb.

"Yes?" Charge put the car in drive, looking like he was ready to end this conversation and get going.

"Never mind."

"Look, Emily, I get that you have doubts, but you need to get over them. Quickly. I don't know how long I can stick around, and the team needs someone organizing these jobs."

She stared down at her small hands. The hands of a killer. "I know."

"Managing this business is no joke. It's life and death every day. I never would have tapped you if I felt you weren't right for the role."

She nodded, still staring at her hands.

"Hey." He reached for her chin, forcing her to meet his gaze. "You never gave a second thought to saving those women from your husband. You knew what had to be done. This job is no different. Every target is an Ed." He paused for a long moment. "If you'd been by my sister's side, she would be alive today. You know that. So think about her if you're getting cold feet. How many sisters are you turning your back on if you don't step up?"

Charge's sister was the elephant in the room

they hadn't really discussed yet. It turned out that Ed's prior girlfriend had been Charge's sister, who disappeared. Emily suspected that Ed had murdered her, threw her off his boat like he usually did when he wanted to get rid of people.

But that wasn't the elephant.

Emily still couldn't figure out how the hell she'd ended up in El Paso, working for Charge. Their connection couldn't be random like he claimed, but on the other hand, *she* chose this city of all the cities in the world to hide. And then *she* answered Charge's classified ad for a job, out of all the jobs in El Paso. It was too fucking weird.

"Fate," she muttered.

"Sure. Maybe," Charge replied, unaware of what she'd just been thinking. "But if you walk away now, it'll be a choice. And cowardice."

"Maybe it's a question of me putting the team first. Maybe I'm not convinced I can keep them safe."

"Emily, I will only say this one last time. They need someone smart, resourceful, and scrappy who can vet these targets with discernment. They need a real human being who can think, who can plan and organize. That person is you. You are the perfect Sampson." He exhaled and shook his head. "And if hearing my opinion isn't enough, then walk away now."

Emily lifted her chin. "I'm finishing the training. I'm doing this." She wanted to prove to herself she could overcome fear. Fear had always been used to control her. She'd allowed people to do bad things to her because of it.

He stared at her with those intense silvery eyes. "You don't sound so sure."

"I don't have a million dollars to pay everyone back for taking down Ed and his awesome group of idiots, and I'm not about to live on the run forever." That had been the very blunt truth after Ed died and the money he had stashed away wasn't found. *Work it off or run.* Charge hadn't left her another option.

"Good choice." Charge flipped down the visor and jerked his head, indicating it was time for her to get out. "I'll be back in a few hours to pick you up and introduce you to your new trainers. Take the time to rest and prepare."

"Prepare for what?"

"Your first job. You start tonight."

Fuck.

CHAPTER THREE

Later that afternoon, Charge drove her to the Rusty Nail, a seedy bar in a run-down strip mall with a sketchy bowling alley and pizza joint. The last time she'd been here, it was during a test. A stress test.

Charge and the crew of suite forty-five had a system of vetting potential operators, which consisted mainly of putting them through multiple deadly situations—being chased by men with guns, a hit job gone wrong, a hostage situation. She'd passed with flying colors, totally unaware she'd been running through a fake labyrinth where the "bad guys" were really part of Charge's team.

Then the worst happened. She was kidnapped. For real.

Because in addition to carrying out hits on specific targets, suite forty-five played a quiet role in pushing back the cartels along the border. Who paid suite forty-five for this, she didn't know, but they frequently took out cartel members. Needless to say, they wanted suite forty-five gone. On that particular day of her kidnapping, Charge's team had been ambushed, and she got caught in the net. They took her. They beat her. They drugged her. Thankfully, Charge got her back in one piece.

Still, the entire nightmare lingered in her mind. This wasn't a game. The stakes were real.

She got out of Charge's car and followed him inside the Rusty Nail. It was a total dive, complete with chipped tables, a cracked concrete floor, way too dim lights, and an old jukebox playing classic country. At the counter, a few loners sat sipping beers and looking at their phones.

"Hey, I brought you a gift," Charge said to a couple seated at a table in the darkest corner of the room.

"Hi, Emily." The woman stood and held out her hand. "I'm Olivia."

They shook hands.

She was a hit man? Or hit woman? Hit person? Olivia looked like she belonged in an accountant's office, kind of your average preppy complete with a tight bun, khaki slacks, and a white cardigan. She couldn't be much older than thirty.

"It's nice to meet you," Emily said and then

turned to the man, who didn't bother getting up. "You must be Flint?"

"The one and only, sweetheart." He gave her a nod. Flint looked a little more the hit man part, with shoulder-length brown hair tucked beneath his baseball cap, dusty black cowboy boots, and arm tats—a snake winding up one arm and an eagle riding an American flag on the other. Strangely, though, he appeared to be even younger than she was. Twenty-one or twenty-two to her twenty-five. He was also good looking and came off as the type who knew it. All cockiness.

Charge stood with his shoulders square and back straight, his presence dominating the room. "Stand up, dickwad, and give Emily a proper greeting."

Flint's brown eyes flickered with annoyance, but he did as he was told. Charge seemed to pull some weight even without anyone knowing he was actually the Sampson.

Flint held out his hand. "Welcome aboard, Emily."

"Uh, thanks." She shook his calloused hand, trying not to think of what his hands were capable of. How many lives had he taken with those hands? Did he have regrets, or was he like Charge?

"Let's get started." Charge pulled out a chair for Emily.

It always surprised her how much of a gentleman Charge was. For example, when she'd been recovering from the cartel's "workout," she'd been pretty out of it. Charge made sure she got medical attention; then he took her to his cabin to recover. When she finally woke up, his biggest concern was for her well-being. He never asked or cared if they'd pressed her for information. He only wanted to make sure she was all right. Other than some major bruises and unwelcome drugs pumped into her, she was okay, thanks to Charge's efforts to rescue her.

"Thank you." She sat and smiled at Charge.

The gesture wasn't missed by Olivia, who raised a blonde brow and smirked.

Charge ignored it and sat. "All right. So here's the deal," he said to Flint and Olivia. "I have to take care of some personal business. I want you both to bring Emily along on the job tonight."

"Tonight?" Olivia's blue eyes went wide. "But it's dangerous as is. We've been given almost no time to make proper preparations, and adding another variable only makes it worse."

"It's fine," Flint said dismissively. "We can handle it. But hey, we want a bump."

Charge nodded. "An extra ten each. That should cover the inconvenience."

"Fifteen." Flint leaned back in the chair, grabbed his beer, and took a swig.

"No," Olivia objected. "This isn't about the money. It's about coming home in one piece. Emily won't know what to do, which means one of us will have to split our attention between babysitting her and the job."

Babysitting? It was Emily's turn to raise a brow.

"Sorry, no offense," Olivia added to Emily. "But this is an eight-two."

"What's an eight-two?" Emily asked.

Charge chimed in. "We have a scale. Easy to difficult. The number of operators is the second factor. The job tonight is an eight—very dangerous—primarily because it's as Olivia just said. There's no time to run through our protocols for prep."

"Why not?" Emily asked.

"We received a tip on a target we've been after for a while. He's rarely out in public exposed so openly, and we can't afford to miss the opportunity. But that's why Sampson is sending in Olivia and Flint. They specialize in dealing with fluid situations."

So the job was considered an eight because they were basically going to wing it? *Oh, great.*

Emily masked her nervousness with a chuckle. "Guess having me along will make it a six-three, then." She pushed back in her chair and looked over her shoulder. "What's a girl gotta do to get a shot of tequila and a cold one around here?"

Flint beamed at Emily. "*I* like her."

"What's that supposed to mean?" Olivia snapped.

He shrugged. "What's up your ass?"

"Nothing," Olivia said curtly. "I just don't want you blowing tonight because you're too busy checking out Emily."

Flint scoffed casually, like nothing could bother him. Ever. "Honey, I never fuck up. And your job isn't worrying about who I'm checking out; it's watching my ass."

Olivia rolled her eyes. "You wish I'd look at your ass. And when have I ever failed to save it?"

Olivia and Flint started bickering about mistakes on past jobs. Emily felt relieved that they were too focused on their little pissing match to notice that she was having a silent meltdown. *Freaking the hell out right now.*

"Enough." Charge stepped in, silencing Olivia and Flint. "Everyone on this team has an obligation to train new operators, especially now that we have seven open positions. Emily is fast, sharp, and tougher than you two clowns. She just needs a little field experience with our team so she knows how we operate, and she'll be ready to go. Solo only."

Olivia and Flint looked at him, eyes wide.

"Solo?" Olivia asked.

"Yes," Charge replied. "Sampson feels she's perfect to take my lineup of jobs, and I agree. Just look at her. No one would ever see her as a threat. She can walk into any public place without raising suspicion."

Emily took that as a compliment. Not looking like a person who killed was definitely a good thing. Also, she was pretty sure that Charge was only saying this because she wouldn't actually be doing many jobs. She would be working behind the scenes. Meanwhile, the teams would think she was off doing solo work, thereby masking the fact that she was the Sampson.

"She'll also be helping him run the office, like I do, and solo work is ideal for that schedule," Charge added. "So the sooner we can get her up to speed, the better off the team'll be. We all know I'm here on borrowed time."

Charge was referring to the fact his cover had been blown with the cartels and they were hunting him. It was time for him to retire and disappear.

"Sure. We'll make it work, Charge," said Olivia.

"And you?" Charge looked at Flint.

"Yeah. Sure."

"Great," Charge said. "I gotta go." He looked at Emily. "A word? Outside?"

She stood and followed him out, wondering how much more unnerving this whole onboarding process could get. Didn't help that it was already hotter than hell. Her nervous sweat was about to get turbo boosters, and soon she'd have a swimming pool in her cleavage.

God, I really want a cold beer. She'd learned to

live without life's little pleasures these past few months—she'd had very little money when she ran from Ed—but tonight, if she survived the job, she was going to buy herself a nice frosty beer. Maybe two.

Once at his car, Charge turned and faced her. "I know you're green when it comes to team jobs, so don't overdo it with the bravado tonight. Take your place at the bottom rung with humility."

"What's that supposed to mean?"

"It means that you don't need to impress them, and you shouldn't try. They can smell bullshit a mile away."

"Then how am I supposed to convince everyone I'm part of the team so they don't suspect I'm Sampson?"

"Leave that to me. In the meantime, listen, watch, and learn. Don't get in their way."

"What will I do on this job?"

"Ask Olivia. She's the lead. She's also the most careful operator we have."

"And Flint?" she asked.

"Nothing scares him, which makes him a little reckless. It also makes him our best asset for extremely dangerous jobs."

Careful and dangerous. Olivia and Flint. That was why Charge wanted her to ride along. She'd see two different sides of the coin.

"If anything goes wrong," Charge added, "listen to Olivia first. She always keeps a cool head."

"What could go wrong?" Emily asked.

"Everything." Charge opened his car door and slid inside. "See you in a few days. Olivia and Flint will get you where you need to go."

"Wait!" Emily's panic took over. Charge was like her training wheels, and he was taking them off before she felt ready. Or was he? Was this another one of his tests? She wouldn't put it past him. *Mr. Mind Fuck.*

"How do I know this isn't one of your fake team exercises?" she asked.

"Because you'll see blood. Likely yours if you screw this up."

Wonderful pep talk. "How do I not screw this up when I don't have actual training? I was never in the military, and I can barely fire a gun."

"But you *can* fire one. And the training is what you're about to get."

Fucking Charge. Has an answer for everything. She glared.

"Emily, you got something to say, then say it. Now's the time."

"I don't want you to go."

He blinked those intense gray eyes at her. "Why the hell not?"

She looked away, too ashamed to admit it.

"Speak. Now or never, Justine."

She snapped her head in his direction. "You know I don't want you using that name."

"Why?"

"It undermines my efforts to stay focused."

He shook his head and slid out from behind the wheel, staring down at her. "Every target, client, politician, law enforcement agent, and cartel member wants to undermine your focus. So get your shit together. Learn how to see the goddamned forest through the goddamned trees, or people will die. The wrong people," he added.

She looked down at her dusty combat boots. She'd found them at a thrift store, thinking they'd help her feel the part. Tough. But what she really needed was this. Charge was pushing her to grow a thick skin, and she appreciated the fact that he thought she could. Her husband had always called her weak. He saw no potential in her. But Charge did. Charge believed she could toughen up. He was the only person she could trust not to judge her past.

"I killed someone," she blurted out, unclear as to why this was coming out of her mouth at this very moment. Maybe she just needed to tell someone.

Charge crossed his thick arms over his chest. "When?"

"After I got on that bus to Denver. There was a man in the women's restroom, and he was trying to—"

"Was it justified?"

She nodded.

"Did you have another choice?" he asked.

It had been late at night, and the man had been holding a knife to a woman's throat one stall over. If Emily had called for help or yelled for him to stop, the man might have decided to do away with the only person who'd really seen his face: the victim. Emily had only seen the top of his head by standing on the toilet and peeking over. It had been a split-second decision, but she knew it was the right one. She took out the gun Charge had given her before she'd left El Paso, after deciding she'd rather run from suite forty-five than become part of their team to pay her debt. She'd hardly known how to use the gun, other than squeezing the trigger, but she drew it and fired. She hit the man right in the head. It was an awful, terrible, gory nightmare, but she'd saved that woman.

"I suppose I could have walked away," she finally answered Charge, "but that wouldn't have been the right choice." The woman would have been raped and probably gotten her throat slit.

"Then it's like I said; you did what had to be done. Don't overthink it. Move on."

Emily got it. She did. But that didn't make her feel any better. Her heart still ached. Her stomach still rolled. Killing was never going to be easy for her.

"Hey." Charge reached out and took her hand, giving it a squeeze. "It'll get easier. I promise."

The warmth of his touch soothed her nerves.

After a lifetime of being set aside, his belief in her was everything.

She looked up, locking eyes with him. Several moments passed, the two staring at each other, while her pulse revved. Charge was so nerve-racking, but at the same time, she'd never met anyone like him. Masculine. Sure. Mesmerizing.

"Don't," he said.

"What?"

"You know what."

Crap, I was just getting all doe-eyed over him. She looked away, feeling her cheeks flush.

"It's not that you're not..." He cleared his throat. "There are rules. Operators cannot fraternize. It's a distraction, and distractions cost lives."

"Sure. Of course." She felt mortified that he'd even picked up on her thoughts. Not that she really wanted him. It was more of an admiration situation.

"Good. Glad you understand. Because there is nothing more important than protecting the team, and you won't be able to do that if you're busy playing favorites." He got back into his car. "Be careful tonight." He shut the door and drove off.

Emily sighed with a heavy feeling in her chest. Charge had just pushed her out of the nest, and whether he admitted it or not, tonight was definitely a test.

Would she pass or die?

CHAPTER FOUR

Olivia and Flint took Emily to what they called the staging box, which was literally a box. Fine, it was a forty-foot metal shipping container near the railyard. Basically, each solo operator or team had one.

"So this whole shipping yard is filled with the team's supplies?" Emily asked Flint as he popped off the heavy-duty padlock.

"These staging areas are all over the place. Some are located in storage lockers or empty apartments. They change frequently, but we still call them staging boxes."

He lifted the sliding lock and opened one of the creaking metal doors. The three went inside, Olivia closing the door with a *thud!* behind them.

Flint hit a switch, and a string of bare light bulbs flickered on across the metal ceiling. A tiny generator, hooked up to a car battery, hummed quietly.

As the scent of turpentine and cleaners hit her nose, Emily tried to hide her shock. Crates were piled up toward the back, but the front area of the container looked like a weapons store, everything neatly laid out on tables—handguns, rifles, scopes, ammo, bulletproof vests.

"Masks and clothing are over there." Olivia pointed to an army green trunk against the wall. "Grab black pants and a long-sleeve shirt. You'll need a set to go in your purse."

Emily scanned the room. There was so much stuff here. It was insane. One table had knifes, compasses, silencers, and weird-looking goggles. Night vision maybe?

"Emily?" Olivia prodded.

"Sorry. What'd you say?"

Olivia pointed again. "There are a couple of big purses in that box over there next to the knives. You'll need to pack your change of clothes in one. I've got a few sundresses in that bag over there."

Sundresses? "What exactly is this job?"

"We are going to a bar in Juarez, Mexico, tonight. You and I will be posing as tourists. Flint will take out the target while we make a distraction. How do you feel about table dancing?"

What the hell? "I feel very bad about it."

"Well, this is the work. Sometimes we play parts. Sometimes we hide in trees. It all depends."

She hated to ask, but, "Who's the target?"

"The man who diced up one of our operators and then ordered the attack on us. Oh, his people are the ones who kidnapped you."

They were going after a cartel member tonight, the one who ambushed Charge and his team? These were not nice people.

"So the target is the big boss?" Thankfully, the ones who actually took her were all dead now. Charge made sure of it.

"The target is the Heroin King's son—runs most of this territory. They call him the Meat Grinder."

"Because he likes to grind people up," Flint added.

"Awesome," Emily said dryly. "Can't wait to meet him." *And pee myself.* This whole thing sounded like a very bad idea, even if she'd like nothing more than to scratch out the man's eyes.

"Are you turning green?" Flint asked Emily.

Olivia leaned toward her a bit, squinting her blue eyes. "She is turning green. See," she looked at Flint, "I told Charge this wasn't a good idea."

Flint shrugged and started fiddling with a handgun, playing with the slidy thing. "She'll be fine. We all get a little nervous before doing an eight. Hell, even a seven fucks with my head. But that's why they're so much fun."

Emily could see what Charge was talking about; Flint was Mr. Danger. Olivia was the cautious one. They made a great team.

"I'll be okay," said Emily, trying to be tough despite Charge's warning not to. "Just tell me exactly what I have to do, and I'll do it."

"That's not how this works," Olivia said. "Jobs like these are fluid. We work on the fly. Our role is to drink, look like we're there to party, and to keep our eyes open to create a believable distraction."

"You mean like 'oops, I dropped my napkin' or a bar fight kind of thing?" Emily asked.

Flint and Olivia exchanged glances.

"What?" Emily asked.

"I have to shoot someone without anyone noticing for three to five seconds so I can slip out the back," Flint said. "Do you really think dropping your napkin is gonna do it?"

"Am I wearing a short dress and no underwear in this scenario?" Emily smiled.

Flint glared. He didn't find her nervous joke funny.

"Sorry. I'm going to stop asking questions now." Emily felt stupid. "Okay, so Olivia and I go in; we create a distraction; Flint shoots the Meat Grinder. What next? And yes, I'm aware that's another question."

Olivia grabbed a hunting knife from the table and inspected the edge. "While our target's bodyguards are distracted by their new unemployment status, you and I run out the front with the rest of the customers. Flint will be waiting around the corner to pick us up. We drive back."

That sounded easy. Too easy. "So what's the dark clothing for?"

"In case we're separated," Olivia said.

Emily stared, not connecting the dots.

"If anything goes wrong, you run," Flint elaborated. "Find a quiet place to lie low for a few hours. Then you cross the border on foot. We can't have any official record of crossing. It's too risky."

Wow. Okay. That sounded fucking terrifying.

"Don't worry; you'll have a wet map to show you the route." Olivia handed Emily a bottle of water. "Put this in your purse. Now chop-chop. Get packed. We still need to go over the bar's layout, the players, and a few other housekeeping rules."

Emily's head was spinning too hard to register that last thing Olivia said. She was expected to hoof it over the border to get home? She hadn't been in El Paso long, but that did not sound awesome. Bad things happened to women traveling alone.

Stop. You're a hit man now. You fear nothing. Emily could do this. She would make Charge proud. Even if it killed her. *Strike that.* Even if it scared her.

Four hours later...

I can't believe I'm doing this. Why am I doing this? Have I lost my fucking mind? Emily never should have come back to El Paso and told Charge she'd take the job. Because this, *this* was not a drill. This was real.

While she and Flint waited in the empty parking garage about a mile from the border, Olivia had gone to pick up some old "clunker and dump her" beige Corolla. She'd just texted Flint that she was almost to them. Showtime.

Don't throw up. Don't throw up, Emily chanted in her head. But the moment she and Flint got inside the vehicle, Emily's head started spinning in the front passenger seat. Then came the rapid breathing.

"Slow inhale. Slow exhale, Emily," Olivia said, putting on her game face along with Flint as they all crossed the border into Mexico. The two looked super chill. All smiles. Emily likely had the expression of a hostage.

"Relax," Olivia commanded through gritted teeth and a smile. "Or I'll dump you at the next corner."

Relax. Relax? On a scale of one to ten, ten being the most dangerous, the job was an eight. *Eight!*

"I'm trying." And how was it that young-soccer-mom here was so tough? She had the expression of someone baking cookies with Martha. Twinkling blue eyes and everything.

"Let's listen to some music. Singing helps sometimes." Olivia flipped on the radio, and an '80s tune came on, "Come on Eileen," by Dexys Midnight Runners.

Emily used to love this music in high school. Disco, too. It always reminded her of the good times, growing up with Aunt Mary. Dad owned a fishing boat and sometimes spent months at sea, so her aunt had been the one to raise her after her mom split. Apparently, Mom couldn't handle the time apart from Emily's dad, so she abandoned her child.

Made no sense.

But Emily couldn't have asked for a better parent in Aunt Mary. She had been there when Dad died, when she had her first boyfriend, and when she triumphantly survived her first heartbreak. Aunt Mary was allergic to pets, but she still let her foster a few cats and encouraged her to pick out a veterinary school for after high school. Mary had been her best friend up until the very end when cancer took her. Emily'd only been seventeen at the time, and her life would change quickly after that—not for the better—but at least she'd always have her memories to look back on. They reminded her that life could be better.

Emily started singing, and Olivia and Flint joined in. *Come on Eileen...*

Emily started to relax, until she noticed the long line of cars heading north in the opposite direction, back toward the US border. "That doesn't look like it'll make for a good escape."

Olivia kept her eyes glued to the busy Mexican city street, which seemed pretty congested for eight o'clock at night. Cars with Mexican plates and strange little buses weaved in and out of traffic. People flowed along the sidewalks, carrying shopping bags or selling stuff in carts. Every other business was a restaurant, T-shirt shop, or taco stand with one of those giant meat cones spinning against an open flame. She'd tried them once at a place in El Paso. Pastor. Delicious.

Emily's stomach grumbled. Like usual, she'd skipped lunch. And breakfast. Eating regular meals had become a luxury lately. She'd lost more weight than she wanted to know. At five-five, she'd already been a little too thin—Ed demanded it—but now she was a freaking wafer. As soon as she earned some decent money, it was cheeseburger city and fresh fruit all day long. French toast and waffles. *Good beer. Oh, God. How I miss good beer.*

"Don't worry about the return traffic," Olivia said. "Focus on the job. We're almost there."

"What if they ask for my passport when we try to reenter the US?" Emily asked.

"You didn't bring your passport?" Olivia's eyes went wide.

Emily felt the blood drain from her face. She didn't have a passport.

"Just kidding." Olivia chuckled. "We have a friend. He'll wave us through."

So one of the border agents was on the suite forty-five payroll? *Interesting.*

Olivia turned down a narrow street jam-packed with clothing shops. She pulled up to the first corner. "This is your stop, Flint. See you in a few."

Now wearing a straw cowboy hat, white button-down shirt, and black jeans, Flint hopped out, not bothering to say a word. He simply walked off, blending in with the people on the street.

"Where's he going?" Emily asked.

"To pick up some local girls. They'll help him blend in. Just remember the housekeeping rules we went over: You don't know Flint. He doesn't know us. Whatever happens in that bar, you don't look at him. Okay?"

Emily's stomach churned hard, twisting her insides into a painful knot. *Fuck. Fuck. Fuck. What am I doing?* Was she really in a foreign country, about to walk into a bar and help kill someone?

Yes. Yes, I am. And it was quite possibly the worst idea ever. Even worse than the time she Ubered to a gunfight, a very ridiculous story best left in the past.

"Here we go." Olivia parked along the curb, several blocks from where they'd dropped Flint, who had a set of keys for later. Olivia made it a point to ensure he put them in his front pocket since he was driving them back, and Olivia would be monitoring the police radios. That seemed to be her primary job—watching out. She also made sure Flint didn't forget stuff. Silencer, cloth to wipe down the gun after he dumped it, cash. No change of clothes for him, though. No backpack. No bags. He said if he carried anything, it would draw attention. Apparently, this Meat Grinder traveled with eight or nine extremely paranoid armed bodyguards. Two stayed by his side at all times. Tonight, the word they'd gotten from some informant was that the Meat Grinder was meeting the local police chief at a bar his brother owned, to deliver a gift. Likely lots of cash. A live band was supposed to play that the Meat Grinder was known to like.

Emily and Olivia exited the car. Olivia gave a few bucks to some guy to keep an eye on it. Weird.

"The bar is just up there," Olivia said.

Emily stared blankly at Olivia. For some reason, her feet didn't want to move. "Maybe I should just stay here with the car."

Olivia scoffed. "No."

"Why not?"

"Because Charge will kick my ass if I don't

take you along."

"I doubt he'd do that," Emily countered.

"Charge is responsible for all training, so disobeying him is like disobeying Sampson."

"And?" Emily asked.

"No one disobeys Sampson. Not if they want to live."

It dawned on Emily that there was another side to the Sampson role: Keeping the team in line. She'd have to talk to Charge about this, because she wasn't about to punish people for disobeying her.

"Emily, could you please wipe that terrified look off your face and smile? We're here to party." Olivia started walking, patting the side of her bun, her knockoff Gucci purse slung over her shoulder. "Let's go."

Emily followed, noting a few guys checking them out. Olivia had on a black mini and low-cut pink tank. Emily wore a super short blue dress. At least she hadn't been forced to wear heels—not conducive to running, should the need arise. Black flats with a good tread was the standard.

Side by side, the two walked through an arched doorway and entered the bar, which was really more of a very large covered patio sandwiched between two buildings. At the far end, there was a stage and some music equipment set up—a guitar, drum set, and mic stand. Most of the white plastic tables were already occupied by people laughing, toasting, and drinking. At the bar counter, off to the side, a few couples crowded together in conversation while three waitresses manned the tables.

"There. That's the perfect spot." Olivia walked over to the table closest to the exit.

Emily exhaled slowly, grateful to have made it through the first part of this job: arriving to the location. Now it was time to drink, pretend to have a good time, and keep an eye out for their target without acting suspicious. The good news was that the Meat Grinder had deep pockmarks on his face, which would make him easy to spot.

Emily took her seat on the white plastic chair with a Corona logo, doing her best not to look terrified, but every time someone walked through the arched doorway, her stomach cramped and her back went rigid.

Meanwhile, Olivia ordered a few beers and kept talking away about absolutely nothing—an article she read, a fight with her nonexistent boyfriend, her terrible boss. Emily had to hand it to her, Olivia knew how to carry on the most boring conversation ever, the sort no one would want to listen in on.

Ohmygod. There he is. The target walked in wearing mirrored sunglasses and a black button-down shirt. Two linebacker-sized men followed closely behind, dressed in suits.

"Where's Flint?" Emily whispered.

"Who?" Olivia asked, an angry warning in her eyes.

"Never mind." Emily had forgotten the rules. Don't get out of character. Don't say names. Not ever.

Emily went back to pretending to listen to Olivia's nonstop chatter; meanwhile her stomach was working into a frenzy. *I really should have eaten something before we left.* "I have to go to the bathroom."

Olivia stopped talking. "Now?"

Emily grimaced. "I'm going to be sick."

"No," Olivia hissed, maintaining a smile. "We have to stay put. You don't abandon your team."

Emily made a little nod of compliance. *Please don't let me vomit. Please don't let me vomit. Please—*

Hot, sour liquid erupted from her mouth. *Oh God!* Emily leaned forward, trying to avoid her clothes.

The bile splattered on the white plastic table in front of her, the smell only making her want to repeat the action. She heaved, knowing everyone was watching her.

Olivia was up and at her side, gripping her shoulder. "Oh no. You drank too much again." She chuckled awkwardly. "Let's get you to the bathroom."

Olivia was staying in character, doing what any good friend might do in this situation.

Emily stood up, cupping her hand over her mouth, trying to hold back further eruptions.

They went toward the back of the patio and inside the small building where the bathrooms were located. Emily pushed her way through the door with the cartoon silhouette of a person in a dress. She dove straight for one of two toilets.

"Jesus, Emily. You've got to be fucking kidding me."

Panting and doubled over, Emily closed her eyes. "I'm sorry. I can't help it."

"No shit."

Another wave of nausea rolled up through her throat, turning into a dry heave. After a few moments, Emily started panting. "I'm sorry. I'm almost done."

"I have to go back out there. Just be sure to listen to what's going on before coming out. Got it? If something's going down, just leave, because we won't wait for you."

In other words, change her clothes and follow the map across the border on foot. *Wonderful.* But she couldn't expect them to risk their lives over her pussy stomach.

"Got it," Emily said.

The door opened and shut, and she was alone with her humiliation and sour stomach. Charge wasn't going to be happy. And when the team found out she'd puked from nerves, no one would believe she was a candidate for solo work, which meant she couldn't be the Sampson. The crew had to believe she was on jobs half the time to account for the behind-the-scenes work.

Feeling a little less woozy, she went over to the stained sink and washed her face, patting herself dry with a scratchy paper towel.

Suddenly, screams erupted on the other side of the door.

She froze. *Oh shit. Flint made his move.* Which meant Olivia was already running out with the other guests. *Shit. Shit. Shit.*

Emily took her bulky purse and went back into the stall. *I can't fucking believe this.* She pulled her dress over her head and dug out her black tee. Next came the black jeans and navy blue baseball cap. The black flats were here to stay.

Okay. Breathe. Breathe. Go to the backup plan. She pulled out the map Olivia had given her.

"You've got to be kidding me." It was blank! Was this some sort of fucking joke? "Motherfuckers."

Emily stashed her dress in the trash, exited the bathroom, and ran past the commotion near the arched doorway. She didn't get a good look, but two feet were sticking out from underneath a group of men huddled over the target. They looked like they were giving him CPR.

Just outside, people were running away down the sidewalk, fleeing the bar. Maybe if she hurried, she could catch up to Olivia and Flint and cross over with them.

Emily walked at a steady pace, trying not to draw attention to herself. People were coming out of the shops to see what the screaming was about. That was good. No one paid any attention to her.

She made a left at the corner and then another left. Two blocks. That was all she had to do to make it to the car.

She got to the next corner only to see Olivia and Flint ahead, pulling away in their beige Corolla.

"No. No. No. No!" Panic took over. She started sprinting, yelling and waving her arms. "Wait! Don't go!" But it was too late.

She stopped at the next corner. A large white SUV with tinted windows came down the street from the direction of the bar. The man driving stopped right in the middle of the intersection. The man in the passenger seat was yelling at him. Were they the Meat Grinder's bodyguards?

The two bickered for a moment, and then one got out, running out into the intersection, looking both ways for any signs of the killer. His partner got out too and began screaming at people walking down the street. She assumed he was asking if they'd seen anything.

The driver marched toward one man in a big hat who was pointing in the opposite direction from where Olivia and Flint had gone.

A relief. No one had seen them fleeing.

Emily realized the SUV was wide open, engine running, while the two men screamed and threatened everyone in a twenty-foot radius.

Olivia and Flint were only a minute ahead. Emily could catch up, flag them down, ditch the SUV, and get the hell out of Dodge.

She sprinted toward the passenger-side door and dove inside, closing the door behind her. She slid behind the wheel and shut that door too, hitting the lock button just as the two men spotted her.

They screamed, waving their arms and stepping in front of her.

Hell no. I'm not stopping. She ducked and kept on going.

They jumped out of the way, pulling guns from their jackets. She heard something hit the back door, but with one turn, she was out of range.

A few blocks later, she spotted signs in English directing people to the border. *Please still be here. Please still be here.* As the SUV approached the lanes, her eyes scanned the long line of cars she'd seen earlier.

There! The beige Corolla was in the far right lane marked for some special pass only. There was one car ahead of them.

"Jesus. Hurry. Hurry!" She hit the gas, accelerating down the lane. The Corolla's bumper came into view just as Olivia and Flint pulled up to the booth.

What do I do? What do I do? They didn't see her.

She hit the horn and waved, smiling like they were old friends.

Flint and Olivia turned around, both of them looking like they'd either seen a ghost or were about to make one. Olivia turned back to the agent to say something.

The uniformed man looked up at Emily, a scowl on his face. Then he waved them through. All of them.

Thank you, God. Thank you. Emily felt like the blood had drained from her body. She was weak, and her vision was spotted. Still, she managed to tailgate Olivia and Flint all the way back to the parking garage, where they'd ditch the Corolla and grab their own cars.

Once there, Emily stumbled out of the SUV, knowing she had some explaining to do. *Or some serious begging.*

Flint charged straight for her, his long hair whipping around as he yelled, "Are you out of your fucking mind? What the fuck, Emily!"

Olivia exited the Corolla, shaking her head in disappointment.

"I'm sorry." Emily held her palms up. "I panicked. I heard screaming. People were running. This SUV was just sitting in the middle of the street, and I thought I could catch up to you before you hit the border."

Flint grabbed her by the collar of her black T-shirt. "I should put a goddamned bullet in your head for this! Do you know how lucky we are that we were allowed to cross? We only paid that agent for one car!"

"I'm sorry. I'm sorry. It was just survival instinct. There was nothing on that map, and I didn't know what else to do!"

"The map? The fucking map? You were supposed to wet it!" Flint gave her another shake.

"Flint, let her go. She didn't mean to do any…any…anything…" Olivia's eyes gravitated toward the back seat of the SUV. "Ohmygod, Emily. What did you do? Whose fucking car is this?"

CHAPTER FIVE

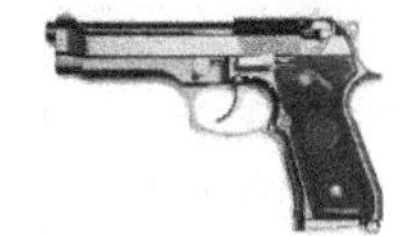

Charge paced back and forth across the empty room that was once the coffee shop section of the bookstore, soon to be the new suite forty-five headquarters. He hadn't said a word since he showed up this morning, pounding on the front door. Emily had been crashing in the back room. There was no shower here, but they had a bathroom and hot water. She'd become the master of the sink shampoo and sponge bath. Occasionally, she rented a cheap hotel room by the laundromat for a proper shower while her clothes washed.

"Say something," Emily muttered, sitting up on the counter next to the espresso machine that had been left behind by the previous owners. She'd already figured out how to use it. Probably not a good idea because the last thing she needed was caffeine in her life. *Tranquilizers. I need tranquilizers.*

"What the hell is there to say?" Charge growled, stopping in the middle of the tiled floor, his eyes lit with fury.

Emily didn't know where he'd just been, but from the looks of it, she assumed it was a formal event. Maybe a family reunion? A funeral? Because Charge was wearing a dark suit on that large, menacing frame of his. He'd also cut his dark hair and shaved off that scruffy beard, exposing his boxy jaw, which was currently pulsing away. He looked like a completely different man. Still dangerous. Still handsome. Just…different.

She, on the other hand, looked like a deranged twenty-five-year-old in her off-brand jeans that didn't fit quite right and a unicorn T-shirt that read *Sparkle Time*. She'd purchased it because it was twenty cents and looked comfortable for sleeping. Sadly, it ended up being her only clean shirt last night after she'd changed out of her all-black escape ensemble.

God, I really need new clothes. Anything that fit right, meant for an adult, would be great.

"Well, for starters," Emily said, "you can tell me what to do."

"What to do?" he snarled. "What to *do!* You just stole a million dollars from the Meat Grinder."

She wrung her hands. "At least he's dead now.

He won't miss it, right?"

A vein popped from his neck. "Wrong! Stealing from him is stealing from the Heroin King. Then you drove right across the border with his drug money, and you almost got two operators in serious shit."

She hopped off the counter. "Like I explained, it wasn't intentional. I reacted. I panicked. I saw the opportunity to get the hell out of there, and I took it. Now, will you please—" she pressed her hands together in the prayer position "—tell me what to do?"

She wasn't sure what the fallout would be for taking drug money from the cartel. Was this the equivalent of declaring war against them? Or was this pocket change they wouldn't miss? She had no clue, given the cash was meant as "a gift" for the police chief, according to Olivia.

"Did the men see your face?" Charge asked.

She bit her lower lip, replaying the scene in her mind. "I don't know for sure. I was already driving away when they noticed me."

He propped his hand on his waist and bobbed his head, mulling.

"So? Do I give the money back? Do I burn it? Are they going to hunt me down?" Maybe if she was lucky, the Heroin King would be too pissed off about his son's execution to notice the missing money.

"Flint got rid of the SUV, so there'll be no

way to trace you through that. And if the men didn't see your face, that helps. You were wearing your hat, correct?"

She nodded.

"Then if you're lucky, no one got a good look at you."

"Well, that's a relief." Emily whooshed out a breath.

"No, not a relief." Charge shook a thick, angry finger at her. He was about to say something but shut his mouth and started pacing again.

She didn't understand why Charge was acting like this. Nothing upset him. He was Mr. Teflon. Maybe there was more going on behind the scenes, and he hadn't told her because he didn't want to pile on the pressure.

"Charge, I'm sorry. I know I fucked up everything on this job, but I can tell Olivia and Flint I had food poisoning or something. We can still sell the solo-operator story." She just needed to figure out how to not let her nerves get the best of her and go on another team job so everyone could see she wasn't a "civilian."

Charge rubbed the back of his neck. "They're not going to buy it. They saw how you lost your shit last night."

So that was it? Game over? She felt like she'd let Charge down. On the other hand, what had she been thinking? She was the last person in the world cut out for this work. "I knew this was a bad idea. I just knew it. I should have walked away when I had the chance."

Charge's voice quieted. "Well, now you can."

Emily blinked, waiting for an explanation.

"You can settle your debt with us," he added. "You can buy your way out with that money you took."

Ohmygod. He's right. She owed suite forty-five a million dollars, and now she had the money. "So…you're saying I can just walk away? Right now? And no one will ever come looking for me?"

"Can't speak for the FBI, but no one from our crew will come after you."

Ed had been an FBI agent, and his disappearance couldn't have gone unnoticed. They'd be looking to question her, which was why she could never go back to her old life. Not that she wanted to.

Charge frowned, staring down like he wanted to say something again. It dawned on her that while this little hiccup solved all her problems, it threw a huge wrench in Charge's world. If she left, he had to stay, which wasn't good for him.

There were three cartels in the area—none of them friends, of course—and they were all looking for Charge. They knew he worked for Sampson, and Sampson had been interrupting their very lucrative business dealings for years. Get Charge, get to Sampson. (Or so they believed, since Charge was Sampson.)

"If I go, what will happen to you and the team?"

"I'll have to set up shop and work remotely," he said. "But I hate to leave the operators here without close support—it's dangerous, and the work never stops."

"Maybe I can help for a while?" she offered, knowing full well she was insane for even considering staying. But pushing back the cartels along the border wasn't the only work the crew had on their plates. They did tons of other jobs all over the country. El Paso was home base because the cartel work required full-time support.

She still wondered who was footing the bill for the work the suite forty-five crew did around here. Maybe the government? Maybe some local business owners? Either way, leaving this team of thirty-eight exposed didn't feel right.

Or maybe something else was making her stomach feel like it had a lead weight inside.

Charge scared the hell out of her half the time. But that was the thing, he scared her in a good way. He pushed her. He refused to let her sit back and play the victim role—something she struggled with after spending years with Ed. But Charge made her see she could be a fighter, not a doormat.

Her biggest problem was she only put her brave panties on when saving other people. That woman in the bus terminal, for example. Then there'd been the woman who she thought was a hostage (really part of the test Charge put her through). She'd even come running to help Charge one time when he claimed he'd been cornered. The point was, Emily only rallied when it was someone else's ass on the line. When it came to her own two butt cheeks, there was this giant fucking wall.

"Did you really just offer to stay and *help*?" Charge said, shaking his head. "I can't figure you out, woman. A week ago, you were whining about having to stay."

He was referring to a conversation they'd had during one of those shooting lessons. "That wasn't whining. It was concern—normal people feelings. Which obviously you don't experience. But maybe you're right; if I stay, I'm never going to be a fit for this."

"What are you talking about?"

"I will run into a burning building to save just about anyone, but when it comes to myself, I can't lift a damned finger." Her eyes teared, though she didn't know why. All she understood was that she had this terrible pain inside. "It's like…" She shook her head. "Deep down, I can't convince myself I'm worth saving. I'm fucked up in the head."

Charge came over and put a hand on her shoulder. "That's not true, Justine."

She winced. She'd told him not to use her old

name. "Why do you keep calling me that?"

"Maybe the problem isn't Emily Rockford or Emily Wilson or whichever name you'll float next week; the problem is Justine Hays, and until you deal with her, you're never going to move on."

Perhaps Charge was correct. She'd started this journey running from her late husband, but even with Ed dead and gone, that life was still managing to follow her. It was in her head, seared into her brain like an ugly cattle brand: *You're weak. You're helpless. You're nothing.* Those were all the things he used to tell her. Now, every day was a struggle to convince herself otherwise. She *could* be a lion. She *could* be strong.

Who the hell am I kidding? "Even if I managed to convince the team I'm one of them, I'd only fuck everything up. I'll make a mistake like I did last night, and next time it'll cost one of the operators' lives." It was strange how much that terrified her. These people were no angels. Sure, they only took jobs involving murderers, pedophiles, and other breeds of dangerous criminals, but that didn't change who the operators were. *Takes an animal to hunt one.*

"This is not a career you prepare for by going to college," Charge said. "There are no manuals. No textbooks. You learn by doing. And yes, you will make mistakes, and it will cost lives. But if you're smart, you'll catch on before leaving a pile of your team's bodies in the road."

She looked away, but he grabbed her by the chin, forcing her to look at him. Typical Charge. He believed in confronting everything head on.

"I'm telling you the truth, Justine. I could train you for ten years, and none of it will teach you faster than getting your hands dirty and knowing that lives are depending on you. I'm sorry it's not a pretty fairy tale. I'm sorry it doesn't come with an employee-of-the-month plaque. But our work is ugly." He dropped his hand.

"I know."

"Then?"

Emily stared into his intense eyes. She could say a hundred different things right now, ranging from how she never went to war, never served in the CIA, hardly knew how to shoot a gun, but none of that mattered to Charge.

"At risk of sounding like a whiny pussy," he added, "why isn't my word good enough for you? I've been through hell and back with men and women who eat bullets for breakfast, and I'm not only talking about suite forty-five. I've fought in Iraq, Afghanistan, and I've even done jobs in countries most people wouldn't be caught dead in. My life has always been about serving and preparing others to serve, no matter how hard it gets. But you," he shook his head at the floor, "you're like a nuclear missile that refuses to accept what it's meant to do."

"I have no experience."

"That is exactly the purpose of training you," he said, his tone growing sharper by the second. "Do you know that most soldiers are only sent to boot camp for a handful of months before they're sent off to war zones? Do you think they feel completely prepared when they're confronted with their first ambush or sniper? Trust me, there is no better teacher than experience."

She stood there mulling, knowing it was time to shit or get off the pot, for lack of a better term. The challenge was, her head was stuck inside the pot, swimming in years of shit. And every time she tried to climb out, she fell back in. This little job across the border was the perfect example. Just when she thought she could handle the pressure. Splash! Toilet.

"I need more time," she said. "I'm not ready to do jobs. And your confidence in me is, frankly, delusional."

"I don't know whether to admire you for your lack of ego or hate you for it."

"Hate. What other option is there?" She flashed an exaggerated, all-tooth smile.

"I can't hate you, Justine. You're far too likeable." His hard eyes softened into something resembling affection. How could a stone-cold killer look at her like that? More importantly, why did she like it so much? Charge could never be more than what he was. Dangerous. Detached. She had to remember that.

So then why was she feeling like this was some big, beautiful moment? She was literally making one kind look from him into something more when she knew it wasn't. Just yesterday, he'd warned her not to go there.

She covered her face. "I can't be this person anymore," she muttered to herself.

"What are you talking about now?"

She dropped her hands, chuckling bitterly at herself. "Never mind." There was no way in hell she'd tell him how good it felt when he looked at her like that. It was the needy pleaser in her, rearing its ugly head again—an old pattern she had to break. "I think my past is just going to keep getting in my way. Like you said."

"That's where you're in luck. With me, you're only judged on one thing: how much you have the team's backs. That's it. You can come from anywhere, be a high school dropout, a complete fuckup, or a decorated soldier. I don't care. With me, you will never be judged for who you used to be. You'll only be measured by your actions."

A few moments earlier, she'd been convinced that splitting town with the money was the best course of action. Now she wanted to stay. Her head was the prison she needed to break free of, and belonging to this team might be the cure. She would have the chance to prove she was strong and capable of handling almost anything. A far cry from who she was a few months ago.

Tears stung her eyes. "I don't want to quit."

"Then don't."

"But you said the operators aren't going to buy the story about me being one of them."

"Maybe not, but we could convince them you're Sampson's assistant. For real this time. We can say that he found your problem-solving talents indispensable, which is the truth."

So Charge found her indispensable. "Does this mean you'll stay, too?"

Charge stared but didn't speak.

"You could be behind the scenes completely," she added, thinking how this made way more sense. Charge cared deeply about the work and the crew. He also had all the experience she didn't. "Having you stay would be best for the team, and you know it. It'll also give me a chance to learn the ropes and earn the team's trust. For when *you* are ready to move on."

Charge rubbed his jaw. She could see the wheels turning. "Only for a few months, until I've really trained you to shoot and fight."

"Really?" He'd said yes. She couldn't believe it!

"Really. Now, if you don't mind, I have an urgent matter to take care of."

"Anything you need me to help with in the meantime?" she asked.

"You could get this place furnished."

"Already happening. I used the cash you gave

me to buy some paintings from a hotel chain that went under. I scored a desk, couch, and a few armchairs, too. If anyone looks in the window, they'll think it's a gallery."

He nodded, pleased. "Then you can get yourself a new apartment in a secure building and some real clothes."

The apartment comment she couldn't argue with, because there was no apartment. She'd abandoned the shithole she'd been renting before. As for her clothes, she couldn't argue with that either. Everything she owned was from the bargain bin at Goodwill. Nothing wrong with secondhand, but if she was really going to help manage this team from this new location, she had to look the part of a manager running a private, appointment-only art gallery.

"I'll get on it."

"You need money?" he asked.

The money he'd already given her went to the deposit, utilities, and furnishing this place. She would have to figure something out. "No. I'm good."

He stared, his eyes flickering with doubt. "I'll give you some, just in case."

"But I don't need your char—"

"It's just a loan. And don't go dipping into that money in the vault. It needs to be cleaned."

"Thank you, Charge."

"Don't mention it." He moved toward the

front door.

"I'm not just talking about the money." It was everything—the way he pushed her, the way he made her think.

He gave her a nod and kept going.

"When will you be back?" Where was he even going?

"I am spending some time with my fiancée before she leaves on an assignment."

What the what? Charge had a fiancée? How did she not know this? "Oh. That's…good. Is she a…CIA or a…never mind. None of my business."

"She's a teacher. She trains farmers in third-world countries on how to get better crop yields."

Of course she'd do that. Of course Charge would be with a woman who was smart and knew how to save the world.

"Impressive," she said, masking her twinge of jealousy.

"She is." He paused. "I also plan to spend a little time in New Jersey."

"Why?"

"I got a lead on your husband's money."

"You've been looking for it?" Charge hadn't said a word about it until now.

"You really think I wouldn't at least try?" Charge sounded annoyed. "I'm out a lot of money."

"Sorry? But why are *you* out?"

"I couldn't let my team go without pay. They

worked hard to clean up the shit your husband left behind, and there were people to pay off to get those women home without piles of paperwork."

"So you…you… You took the money from your own pocket?" She couldn't believe it.

"After you agreed to stay, I felt it was the best option." Charge looked away.

Ohmygod. He'd paid off her debt. "Why didn't you tell me?"

"Don't get the wrong idea. I didn't do it for you. I did it for my team." His gaze hardened. "And I believed you when you said your husband had money stashed away. In my mind, it was just a question of time before I found it."

She couldn't remember anyone doing anything so selfless for her. "Thank you."

"Like I said, I did it for the team. Maybe for myself, too. I figured you'd have an easier time earning everyone's trust if you didn't owe them money."

Maybe that was the truth. Maybe there was more to it given how secretive Charge was when it came to the inner workings of the business, but now wasn't the time to address it. There was work to be done.

"I have to go," he said. "I'll let you know if I find that money."

"You're still going to look for it?" She didn't know why. They were square now. Charge had his money back—the cartel cash in the safe—and the team had been paid.

"Yes."

"Why?"

"Until you start pulling your weight, you won't get paid. And you need to live off something." He turned and left.

He was doing it for her.

But why?

CHAPTER SIX

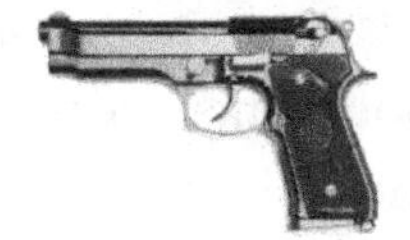

This time, Charge sent money directly to her Zelle account. The alert on her phone said she'd received ten grand. It was a lot of cash, at least for her. But the gesture drove home a few worrying facts.

Ten thousand dollars was apparently peanuts to a man like Charge. And the way he so easily parted with his hard-earned cash meant that he either (A) wasn't in this for the money or (B) the money bothered him, as in, he literally didn't want it. Blood money. Would she inevitably feel that way, too, once she started getting paid for jobs?

Either way, suite forty-five was extremely profitable. She'd already seen some of the older job files when she'd been at the old headquarters a few miles from here. According to the pay sheets, the operators always got their cut, but "Sampson" (i.e., the House) got his, too. Sometimes more, sometimes less, depending on the amount of work that went into the planning and the overhead— guns, ammo, rental cars, hotels, bribes, etc.

But now that she'd decided to stay a while, she'd spent the last twenty-four hours thinking long and hard about what *she* wanted out of this.

Where was this going?

Was she in this for the money?

It wasn't like she'd run around risking her neck for free while the operators were paid twenty thousand or more per job.

Okay, so she wasn't going to treat this like a charity. But to say that the money was enough to motivate her was a lie. She couldn't put her heart into this if she didn't believe she was helping people who'd been left behind by the world, by justice, by the system.

So what did she really want?

Revenge?

To rid the world of Eds who profited from stealing women who were drugged and raped ten times a day?

Was it knowing that justice would be served to the priest who molested hundreds of children, the CEO who polluted the drinking water of thousands of people, including children, or the politician who made backroom deals so his corrupt family could cash in?

All. Of. The. Above. She didn't want those

kinds of people having free rein over this world. People who took everything and left you hollow, like Ed had done to her. She hated the fact that he'd kicked her so many times that she hardly felt pain anymore. What the hell had kept her going all those years?

She didn't know, but maybe it was like her aunt Mary used to say: *There are two paths in this life, Justine. One ends, and one doesn't.*

She used to think it meant what doesn't kill you makes you stronger. But maybe the true meaning was something else. Most people lived and then they died. End of story. The world went on as it always had. But others chose to leave a mark that carried on long after they'd gone.

So maybe that was what she wanted: to change some small piece of this world forever. Didn't matter if she got the credit, but if she could look herself in the eye every day and know she was doing more with her existence than sucking up good clean air, that would be enough. If she got to throw in a few Ed-headstones, even better. Not being dirt-ass poor would be great, too. She couldn't remember the last time she ate a thick juicy steak or bought a new pair of shoes that came with a box.

But first things first. Gotta have a safe place to live. Emily's eyes swept the modest studio with freshly painted light gray walls and new beige carpets. The tiny kitchen had granite counters and a real stove. There was even a balcony where she could sit outside and read or drink coffee. Maybe she'd get a plant baby. The complex was clean with security cameras, an iron gate to drive in and out of, and three separate entrances—all of them requiring a keycard to enter. Safe.

It feels like a dream. Definitely a step up from junkyville where she had her last place. Also this studio was just a few minutes from the "art gallery" and had one of those fancy health food stores down the street. Soon she could afford those fancy green smoothies for breakfast. *Or buy real groceries. I'd settle for that.*

"Sorry for the interruption." The building manager, a blonde in her thirties, popped her head in. She had stepped out into the hallway to answer a call. "So what do you think?"

Emily loved it. "I'll take it."

"Wonderful. You can come down to the office and fill out the paperwork. I just might be able to get you approved before I leave at three if I hurry."

It was almost eleven in the morning. Could she actually have a home by dinnertime? "Great."

They both exited the studio. Emily hoped to God this was the right decision. Staying in El Paso meant getting in deeper. But if she really, truly wanted her life to change, it would take something like this. Go figure. The cure for Ed was working for a group of hit men. *Drastic cure for a drastic illness.*

But she'd made up her mind. She was staying. Next on her list of to-dos for the day was buying that hair dye and clothes. At the moment, she had on yesterday's jeans and a really horrible pink polyester blouse with frilly lace on the collar she'd found buried at the bottom of her duffel bag. She'd forgotten she had it. On purpose.

Her phone rang. The number was private.

"Hello?"

"It's Olivia."

Why would she be calling? "What's up?"

"They have Charge."

Huh? Emily looked at the apartment manager. "Sorry. I'll be right behind you. I need to take this."

"No problem." The woman walked down the hallway toward the elevators.

Emily waited until the woman was out of earshot. "Who? Who took him?"

"And therein lies the question."

"Whoa. Whoa. Hold on. How do you know someone's got him? Are you sure?" Emily headed for the stairwell.

"Because he and I were supposed to meet before he caught his flight."

"And?"

"And he never showed up," Olivia said.

A sliver of hope bubbled in Emily's chest. "Well, he probably just forgot or something. I know he's been super bus—"

"You haven't been fully trained as an operator for our team yet, and maybe you never will, considering the shitshow the other night, but if you had, you'd know the rules. One being that we never miss appointments, meetings, or jobs. We live by the clock. Especially when we're coordinating complicated jobs where precision is everything. If something comes up, we call Sampson. Sometimes he asks for a code word so he knows we're not in distress."

"Okay, but maybe Charge forgot?"

"Do you know Charge?" she growled.

"Yes."

"Then you know how fucking ridiculous you sound right now."

Olivia was right. Charge wasn't forgetful. Not even a little.

"The worst part is," she added, "that Sampson is MIA."

Of course he would be. "So you called him and no answer?" Emily asked, wanting to hear what Olivia might say.

"I got his usual recording for when he's out on a job."

"What does it say?"

"If Sampson doesn't respond in six hours, we're supposed to call Charge."

Fuck. Why would Charge tell the team to call him if he (Sampson) was missing?

"So what do we do?" Emily asked.

"Let's cut the bullshit, okay? I know Sampson has a hard-on for you. Otherwise, he wouldn't have brought you on board to be an operator—a job you're clearly not cut out for. And we all know you're helping him run the office."

Okay. Fine. She wasn't a cutthroat killer. Not a crime. Literally. Still, she was the kind of person who stepped up when it mattered most. "What's your point?"

"You know where Sampson is. Probably off fishing again or on another cruise."

Is that what they all thought Sampson did when he took time off? Weird. "Well, I don't know, but I really wish I did." More importantly, she really wished she knew where Charge was. "Do you have any idea who took Charge?"

"Um…let me fucking guess," she said condescendingly. "Could it be, perhaps…the assholes you stole a million dollars from!" Olivia yelled.

"But they didn't see my face. I drove away before—"

"Yeah, genius. That's the problem. If they *had* seen you, they'd be after you. Not him! But no. You had to jump in their SUV and take off, leaving them to conclude the only person who would possibly fuck with them like that is Sampson. Of course, they don't know who the hell Sampson is, so they upped their search for the one person they know is connected to him."

Charge. Of course.

Emily let out a long groan, pushing her fingertips through her two-tone hair. Hair that was long overdue for that chestnut touch-up.

Why the hell am I thinking about my hair? The likely answer was that she didn't want to think about those cartel men torturing Charge. They had zero compassion. The men she'd come across were animals who'd reveled in her pain.

"I don't know what to do." Emily groaned her words.

"You need to get a hold of Sampson. You need to tell him to gather everyone up and trigger whatever protocol he has for this situation."

Oh God. What do I do? Unlike before, this wasn't a test. And if Olivia and the rest of the operators were all waiting for a nonexistent person to tell them what to do, then Charge was screwed. Really, truly screwed. She had to do something, but only one solution popped in her head. It was the sort of thing Charge would not be happy about if he survived. *Cross that bridge when I get there.* She had no other choice.

"There is no Sampson," Emily blurted out. "He's a façade. A cover. Charge is the man—" she winced "—in charge."

Olivia burst out laughing, forcing Emily to pull the phone from her ear. "Yeah, and I'm Oprah. You get a car, and you get a car and—"

"Stop. I'm serious. Charge is Sampson. He's

been training me to take his place so he can retire."

A long pause ensued.

"Now I know you're lying," Olivia snarled. "You're about the worst leader I've ever seen."

"Thanks. I appreciate the vote of confidence, but can we table your enthusiasm for a moment so we can focus on getting Charge back in one piece?"

Olivia went silent for a long moment. "You're goddamned serious, aren't you?"

"Why would I lie?" More importantly, why would she tell Olivia the truth about Sampson, betraying Charge's trust, if it weren't a matter of life or death?

"How should I know? Have you taken a hard look at our team? Not like any of us have ever received the honesty award."

Emily stepped outside, exiting the building from the stairwell. *Bye, beautiful studio.* All that would have to wait. "Okay. You don't believe me. So Charge isn't Sampson. And Sampson conveniently isn't answering his phone when Charge has been taken. And I'm not here trying to learn the ropes because Charge tried to convince me I would be a good coordinator for this team." She threw a hand in the air. "So why don't you tell me what to do, since you clearly have all the answers?" Emily heard a break in the line.

"Hold on," Olivia said.

The call went silent.

"Hello? Olivia?" Had something gone wrong?

"Hey, Emily," Olivia said, coming back on the phone. "Guess who just called me? Sampson. And he wants a word with you, you fucking liar."

Emily's blood ran cold. What the hell was going on? "You mean, you just spoke to him? Sampson. *The* Sampson."

"Yeah, genius. Meet him at the Rusty Nail. Twenty minutes. And if I were you, I'd bring my groveling pants."

"Groveling pants?"

"In our business, it's called a Hefty bag."

Oh crap. What was going on?

CHAPTER SEVEN

Lies upon lies upon lies was all Emily could think when she pulled up in her ride, around eleven thirty in the morning, to the Rusty Nail. Unarmed. Unhinged. Unwilling to accept that Charge had sold her a bag of bullshit.

Was there a real Sampson?

Her gut always told her she'd been too hasty to believe everything Charge said. His stories never added up completely, but she'd convinced herself it was because he played it close to the vest. Why wouldn't he? Hit man and all.

She thanked the driver and hopped out, waiting several moments before taking that first step toward the door.

Inside that dump of a bar were the sort of answers she wasn't sure she wanted to hear. Her head and heart couldn't take knowing that Charge wasn't who he said. She'd been let down by almost everyone she'd ever known, aside from Aunt Mary. Charge was the one person she looked up to, who was still alive, anyway.

Fuck. Let's do this. Band-Aid time. She marched to the creaky wooden door and jerked it open. *I can't believe I'm meeting Sampson, wearing a hideous frilly pink blouse.* She hadn't meant to buy it, but the thing had been on the infamous bargain rack along with a few other shirts, and she'd been in a hurry that day to meet up with Charge for their shooting lessons.

Emily stepped inside the run-down bar, taking a moment to adjust to the dark smoky room. In the corner, a doughy man wearing a black jacket and baseball cap sat with a beer mug in front of him.

There was no one else in the bar aside from the bartender, who never seemed to pay attention to anyone unless they were at the counter asking for a drink. Other than that, he kept his head down. *Part of the Rusty Nail's charm, no doubt.*

"You must be Sampson," she said, walking over to the man.

He nodded. "Have a seat, Emily."

Her hackles rose. Whoever this man was, he knew her cover name. Could this really be Sampson?

She took the seat across from him at the small, chipped table. Her eyes hadn't adjusted to the room, but the man appeared to be older—

wrinkles around the eyes and lips—with a black mustache and beard.

She stared, resisting the urge to let loose with her questions. *Better let him do the talking.* If he wasn't the real Sampson, he might tip his hand. "Okay. So, I'm here."

"Would you like something to drink?" His voice was unnaturally gravelly, like he had an issue with his vocal cords.

"No, thank you. I don't drink before wine-thirty. Just tell me what you want."

"The answer to that depends on you. What do *you* want, Emily?"

What kind of game was he playing? "Care to elaborate?"

He leaned his round body back in his chair. She wasn't judgy when it came to body types, but if he really was Sampson, she found it strange that he'd be so out of shape. From everything she knew about running suite forty-five, it was a very physically demanding job.

She waited for him to speak as he fiddled with his phone, flicking his finger on the surface. What was he doing?

Finally, he placed the device facedown on the table and flashed a snide smirk. "Let me ask you, Emily, how much do you value your team's lives? Or yours? What are you willing to do to save them?"

What the hell? "Who are you? Because I know

you're not Sampson."

"I represent a group of individuals who have business interests along the border."

Ah. Here we go. Now this made way more sense. "So you're cartel."

"No," he replied bluntly.

She almost felt relieved. "Then?"

"Let us simply say that I have something you want, and you have something I want. How's that sound?"

Emily hated when people spoke in circles. Did they think it made them sound scary or smart? To her, it just meant they were trying to hide something. *Like being a jackass.*

Emily folded her arms over her chest. "The faster you tell me what you want, the faster I can give you an answer."

He flipped the phone over and slid it closer to her so she could see the photo on display.

"Jesus!" She covered her mouth. It was Charge. His face was bloody, eyes swollen. He was tied to a chair.

Olivia was right. Someone had him.

Emily urged herself to stay calm while images of being punched and chained to a post flashed in her head. It was Charge who came to get her. Charge and a few members of suite forty-five.

"What do you want?" She balled her fists under the table.

"Full control back."

"Of what?" she asked.

His brows bunched together, like he wasn't sure if she was joking or not. "Charge didn't tell you?"

"Guess not."

"The border used to be our territory before Sampson came along and edged us out."

Oh. Ohhhh… "You're a group of—"

"Private security. At least, that's what we like to call it."

Holy crap. So not only did suite forty-five have the players to the south who wanted to kill them, but there was a rival group of hit men, too? Did the drama ever stop around here?

"I'm sorry." She cleared her throat. "But I'm fairly new to *private security.* How did you lose this 'customer' to begin with?"

"That's not important, but here's what is: You tell Sampson he has twenty-four hours to inform your clients that you're no longer providing service in this area and permanently vacate the states along the border. In exchange, we won't kill Charge. And in case Sampson's thinking he can live without him, we've been doing our homework. We know who ten of your operators are now. We know where they live. Where they eat. Where they shop. Sampson has been getting sloppy at protecting his people." He shook his head and tsked. Then he went to his phone and tapped again. Up popped a photo of Emily with

Flint and Olivia, heading into the shipping container the other night.

Fuck. Charge had probably been too occupied with her and trying to stay out of the cartel's hands. He hadn't been sloppy. He had been spread too thin, and part of it was her fault.

"All right." She slowly folded her hands on top of the table while her leg bounced beneath it. "We leave the border. Sampson gets Charge back—in one piece, alive, and no additional bumps or bruises. Is that all?"

He smiled, flashing a set of overly white teeth that seemed to glow in the dark, reminding her of the Cheshire cat. "No. Tell Sampson he still owes me my money."

Oh God. "How much?"

"He knows."

"Look, buddy, this feels like a fairly important term to your deal, so I'd rather not leave anything open to interpretation. Sampson is a very busy man."

"Two million."

Emily winced on the inside. *Sonofabitch. Really?*

She plastered a smile to her lips. "Okay, I'll let him know." She stood, using every ounce of willpower not to shake or trip. This was bad. How did she always manage to end up in the middle of this crap?

Wait. "What made you contact *me*?"

"Charge. He said you're the new gatekeeper."

Gatekeeper? "And how'd you get Olivia's number?"

He chuckled at her, like she was dense. "Only took a few broken fingers for Charge to give up the password to his phone."

Dear Lord. This couldn't be happening. "How do I get a hold of you?"

He placed a business card in the middle of the table. The name said Mr. Dearheart. Ironic name for a man who had no heart and likely wasn't dear to anyone.

She shoved the card in her pocket. "I'll be in touch." She turned to leave.

"Oh, and, Emily, I'd watch my back if I were you. The Heroin King is very unhappy about you helping yourself to his money. I hear one of his friends obtained video footage of you crossing the border with his SUV."

This time, she couldn't hide her emotions or stomach cramps. Or racing heart. No doubt she was turning green.

He added with a smile, "You didn't actually think you'd walk away with all that money, did you?" He shook his head again. "Sloppy. Sloppy. Word of advice, men like him have eyes and ears everywhere—especially in Juarez. Every street corner, every laundromat, every liquor store. You can't take a piss in his town without him knowing. And, woman, you took a shit right on his doorstep, starting when you helped execute his son."

She smiled tightly, but only to avoid screaming in hysterics. "Thanks for that very vivid metaphor. Are you a poet on the side, Mr. Dearheart? Or is that one of your torture tactics?"

His glib smile melted away, and he tapped his finger on the table. "Twenty-four hours, Emily."

She nodded.

"I'll tell Charge you send your regards," he added.

His words were a not-so-gentle reminder that she should watch her mouth. Charge's life hung in the balance. "Thanks."

She was almost to the door, tears welling in her eyes, when Dearheart threw out one last thing, "Oh, and after this is over, if you ever change your mind about working for Sampson, we might have a place for you. Charge says you're his best asset. I can see why."

She didn't bother to ask what he meant or even turn her head to acknowledge his parting words. Instead, she pushed on the door and kept walking until she was at the bus stop a block away. She sank down onto the bench, next to a young guy who was wearing earphones.

She covered her face and bawled. *This isn't happening.* But hadn't she learned her lesson by now? It *was* happening. It was always happening.

God, I swear, if this is another of Charge's tests, I'll murder him myself.

CHAPTER EIGHT

"No. No way. I don't believe you." Olivia shook a finger at Emily, her blonde ponytail whipping back and forth as she jerked her head. "And what the hell are you wearing?"

Emily sighed and then turned to Flint, who sat slouched next to the espresso machine on the counter, looking like the world's most laid-back cowboy. Something had him occupied on his phone.

"Flint? Do you believe me?" Emily hoped to God that someone did.

He shrugged, too absorbed in whatever he was doing.

Emily walked over and smacked the device from his hands. It tumbled to the tile floor. "I'm talking to you."

His brown eyes slowly lifted from his now empty palm. "You touched my phone."

"I'll touch your face if you don't pay attention." Emily raised her voice and said, "Charge's ass is on the line. I saw a picture of what they did to him."

Flint hopped off the counter and grabbed his phone from the floor, inspecting it for damage. "That's our business, darlin'. We kill; we get killed."

And she thought she was fucked in the head. "What is the matter with you? Charge would never leave you to rot with those people."

Flint chuckled smugly. "He's an operator. He saves asses when Sampson makes him, but only then."

Olivia chimed in with a chuckle of her own. "Well, Emily here seems to think that Charge is Sampson."

A sharp laugh ripped from his mouth. "Yeah. Sure. Charge is the legendary Sampson."

"Why not?" Emily snapped, placing a fist on her side.

"Because Charge joined our team a couple of years ago, and Sampson has been around forever."

"Forever?" Emily narrowed her eyes, calling bullshit on his hyperbole.

"Well, a long time, anyway," Flint corrected.

"I get why you don't believe me, but ask yourself why Sampson would make me run the gauntlet to become part of the team? I had to pass every single test you guys threw at me, which I did. But you all saw how I was the other night on that job. I could barely breathe, let alone help you put a bullet in that Meat Slider's head."

"Meat Grinder," Flint corrected. "And so what? You're good at the supporting role, something Sampson's been pretty open about."

"No. No! You're missing the point." Emily shoved her hands in her hair and tugged at her roots. She was about to lose her shit. "Charge *is* Sampson. Only now, Charge can't be him anymore because Charge blew his operator cover when your team member got nabbed. He asked me to step in and be the new Sampson because he thinks I'd do a good job coordinating. Leave the actual killing to the pros.

"The only problem was convincing you guys I'm an operator, because no one can know who Sampson really is, and there had to be a reason for me to be involved with the team."

Flint and Olivia exchanged skeptical glances.

"All right." Emily threw her hands in the air. "Then I guess I'll have to get Charge back on my own, while you clowns stand around wondering why Sampson is MIA."

"He just called me. You were there." Olivia shook her head.

"That was the guy I just told you about. Mr. Dearheart. He has Charge's phone. And Charge uses some app to mask his voice when he's being Sampson, so that guy used it, too."

"Dearheart?" Flint repeated and then looked at Olivia.

For the first time, Olivia's smirk dropped. Her body language shifted from relaxed to rigid—straight back, arms crossed over her chest protectively. "This isn't good."

"So you know who he is?" Emily felt hopeful this would lead to getting Charge back.

"Kind of," Olivia replied. "I mean, I've heard of him. He's the kind of guy anyone can hire for any job. You just have to be willing to pay."

"So who hired him?" Emily asked.

"Probably the Warren Group," Flint threw out. "It's a family-run business. They used to *protect*," he made air quotes, "the border, but it was more of a shakedown business model. Maybe Dearheart works for them now."

The three fell silent for a moment, everyone staring at the tile floor.

"Okay." Olivia exhaled and looked at Emily. "Let's say you're telling the truth. Charge is Sampson. But that doesn't solve anything, because I can tell you right now, Sampson—Charge—whatever—would never run from El Paso. He wouldn't sell out this town or any of the towns who depend on us. Not for anything. Especially after all the crap we went through to kick out the Warrens."

Flint added, "Letting them take control again would be like electing the Heroin King as the mayor of El Paso. Hell, make it the governor of Texas. Warren answers to whoever pays the most, and it's usually whichever cartel has the deepest pockets."

Emily scrubbed her face with her hands. *Jesus.* What was she going to do? What would Charge want her to do?

She dropped her hands with a huff. "I don't get it. You two are saying that Charge wouldn't run. So why would he pull me into this when he knows I would try to save him and comply with Dearheart's demands?"

"Because Charge is not Sampson," Olivia said. "And for the life of me, I don't know why he'd try to convince you he was."

Emily could start having doubts at this moment, but she'd been on a call with the entire team when Charge had used several devices to be both Sampson and Charge. The entire point was to always protect Sampson's identity because he was the glue that held everything together.

"Fine. Okay." Emily bobbed her head. "If you two don't believe me, I can live with that, but Charge can't. Will you at least contact the team and tell everyone to take cover? Just for a week?" At least then she could pretend they'd complied with the order from Dearheart.

"We don't know how." Flint grabbed the hem of his cowboy-style shirt and started polishing his phone. "Only Sampson knows."

Olivia cleared her throat and looked at Flint. "That's not entirely true."

"Are you crazy?" Flint said, his voice pure male condescension. "What's the rule, huh? What's the goddamned rule?"

"I know the rule," Olivia snarled back. "I know them all. That's my job. But Sampson put the Flower Pot in place for a reason."

"Flower Pot? What's the Flower Pot?" Emily asked. Charge had never mentioned it.

"It's a website we all have access to. It's a fake florist site, and depending on what flower is displayed on the home page, we know if something's up."

Weird. But okay. "So you can tell everyone to vacate?"

"We could," Flint said. "But it'll cost ya."

No. Please don't ask me for money. Please? "How much?"

"I'll do it for ten."

Emily groaned and pulled out her phone to access the money Charge had given her for an apartment and clothes. "What account do I transfer the money to?"

"Emily, I was joking." Flint paused with a cocky smirk. "But nice to know you have spare lunch money lying around if I ever need it."

She dropped her hand. "Guys, this isn't funny. I'm trying my best to help this man, and you don't seem to care."

Flint continued smirking. "That's the thing, Red—and yes, we all know you're a redhead—your drapes are showing. But the jubilance of your need to rescue Charge raises suspicion. I mean, you hardly know the guy, right?"

"Unless there's more going on." Olivia raised a blonde brow. "Are you two fucking?"

Emily's eyes opened wide, reminding her it was time to take out her uncomfortable brown contacts. She only wore them today to hide her green eyes so her ID would match when she went apartment hunting. The driver's license of Emily Wilson said brown eyes.

"No. Charge and I aren't fucking. He helped me. He gave me a job when no one else would. That's it."

Olivia and Flint stared with skepticism.

"Why would I jump into a relationship? You both know about Ed. You were on the team that—"

Olivia raised her hand. "We never discuss jobs. Not after. It's in the rules."

"Well, I wish someone would share the rules with me," Emily yelled. "Because I'm trying to get you guys out of town before this asshole kills almost half the team along with Charge as well. Oh, and by the way, you're in that half. Dearheart says he knows at least *ten* people's identities, and three are in this room. He showed me a photo of us entering that shipping container the other night."

"Why didn't you say so?" Olivia asked.

"I didn't think I had to be more specific than 'they will kill us if we don't get the hell out of here.' Please, guys, you don't have to believe me about Sampson, but at least help me tell the team to stay away."

"What about Charge?" Olivia asked.

Now she cares? "I don't know." Emily rubbed her forehead.

"Do you still have the five-finger discount from the other night?" Flint asked.

"You mean the money I accidentally stole from Meaty Man? It's back in the vault. Charge never got a chance to clean it."

"Okay. This is good," Olivia said. "We give Dearheart that money and find a way to pull together another million."

How was that good? A million was a ton of money. At least Olivia and Flint were coming around. "Do either of you have access to that much cash?"

"Sorry, but we're not drug dealers. We invest, have offshore bank accounts, a vineyard in Italy," Flint added.

"Nice to know." Emily hung her head. "Where the hell am I going to get the rest?"

"Your husband," Olivia said. "Charge never had a chance to find the money."

"You guys know about that?" Emily asked.

"What? That he took on your debt?" Olivia shook her head. Apparently, she didn't agree with Charge's decision.

"Pussy move." Flint clicked his mouth. "But hey, it was his money to gamble, not ours. We got paid in the end."

This didn't make sense. They acted like Charge was disposable, yet they knew he was the type of guy to bend over backward to make sure they were made whole.

That said, there was no other option to get her hands on so much money. They had twenty-one hours to get everyone out of town and pay up. *Oh, and…* "Do either of you know how to tell our clients there's a new sheriff in town?" That had also been one of Dearheart's demands.

Olivia and Flint started laughing.

"What?"

"Yeah," Flint said, "we stop showing up. The jungle will take over all on its own."

Emily didn't like the sound of it.

She drew a deep, deep breath. The chill setting in her bones told her this was all going to go terribly wrong. But what else could she do? Leave Charge to die?

At least we have half the money, safe in the vault. And getting the team out of town was easy. Now all they needed was to come up with a second enormous pile of money. Money she swore she'd never touch, never use, never want. It was the dirtiest kind of money. Money *he* made doing the unthinkable to those poor women.

But all that was history now. She couldn't undo Ed's sins. She could only try to save the one man who'd been there to drag her out of the mental mud.

And not get caught while saving him. Going anywhere near her old house was a risk. Everyone knew Ed—every cop, restaurant owner, politician. If anyone said they weren't aware of his side business, they were lying and just looking the other way. Sure. Okay. Maybe they didn't know everything, but they knew Ed was the sort of man you shouldn't mess with. By now, people had surely noticed his disappearance. And hers. If anyone spotted her, there'd be questions.

"Okay." Emily clapped her hands together. "Who's ready for a trip to New Jersey?" She looked at Olivia, then Flint. They both lowered their eyes to the floor. "Seriously? You guys judge me for throwing up at a bar in Juarez, but now you're staring at the damned floor?" They looked like a couple of high school students avoiding the math teacher.

"Look, darlin'." Flint whipped out a toothpick from his shirt pocket and popped it in his mouth. "I got places to be. Things to do."

Asshole.

"And you?" Emily looked at Olivia.

Olivia's expression was more apologetic than

Flint's. "I'm sorry, but I have enough on my plate."

"I swear, I've never met a group of more opportunistic, shallow—"

"Keep goin' with the insults, sweetheart." Flint reached toward the back of his jeans.

Emily raised her hands. She'd forgotten whom she was talking to. Hit man. Hit woman. Hit people. Whatever. They were hired guns. Money spoke. Nothing else. It didn't matter what Charge had said about suite forty-five being a team who only judged each other on how much they protected one and other.

"What if…" Emily hesitated, knowing this could backfire, "I find more than a million in Ed's stash? If you help me find it and get it to Dearheart before his deadline, you can keep it."

"That's a hell no from me, sweetheart." Flint took his toothpick and flicked it at her. "I ain't dumb. And I ain't crazy."

"But you're greedy," Emily threw back. "And Ed was raking in an average of ten to twenty thousand a week for three years before I left him. I saw some of the deposits before he whisked them away." Emily waited, letting the math sink in. By her calculations, there could be another million on top of the money she needed. "So are you in?"

"What's the collateral?" Olivia asked.

Not this again. "Nothing. It's all on your dime. It's your risk. Whatever we find above the million is yours. If it's less, that's your problem."

"And you want nothing out of this?" Flint narrowed his brown eyes.

"No." Emily just wanted to get Charge back. Like he'd done for her.

Flint and Olivia exchanged glances.

"My partner and I accept," Flint said.

Emily sighed with relief. "I'll book the tickets." *And change my underwear.* Maybe she'd buy some Depends on the way to the airport. She would have to get into her old house and confront her memories, her old life, and the dark closets she'd once been locked in. She'd have to relive the pain she'd endured inside those four walls, all to look for clues as to where Ed hid his money.

She didn't know if she could mentally survive this trip, but if she did, she could only hope that Charge was worth it.

A one a.m. arrival to Newark was the earliest flight Emily could find from El Paso. So, in order to get back in time, they'd have to catch the six a.m. flight. That would get her to the Rusty Nail just before the eleven-thirty deadline. Unfortunately, that only left them with five *very* short hours to get into her old house, search the place, and hopefully find clues to where the money was hidden. Which could be multiple places. Ed was an asshole, but no fool. He wouldn't have left his money in one place, like stashing it inside a mattress. No, he worked for the FBI. He would've known how to hide the money well.

That was where Olivia and Flint would help. Between the three of them, they could cover more ground. The only way this plan didn't pan out was if Ed had used safe deposit boxes under fake names. Then she was screwed. Because it wasn't like he would've put her name as an account holder. If anything, Ed would've added Merrill, his equally corrupt brother. He was dead, too. The entire group involved with trafficking those women had been hit. That was why suite forty-five had charged so much. The job entailed getting rid of a lot of bodies, not to mention getting those poor women to the right people who could help them.

Emily boarded the plane alone. She'd booked three roundtrip tickets with different seats, knowing it was a risk being on one flight. Easier to tie them together, should anyone ever go looking. But this was one of those situations where risks had to be taken. Proof being that she could be spotted by a nosy neighbor the moment she entered her old house.

With the help of a sleep aid, Emily napped, only to be woken by the plane landing, immediately triggering her flight-or-fight response—rapid heartbeat, sweat everywhere, and fast breathing. She felt like her chest was about to cave in.

With weak knees, Emily disembarked, grabbed a PowerBar from the newsstand in the terminal, and headed straight for the rental cars. Flint and Olivia would travel in two separate vehicles and meet her behind a gas station a few miles from her old house. Because the other two were unfamiliar with her home, it was up to her to go through any possible hiding places where Ed might've hidden records.

Forty minutes later, Emily pulled through the front gate of the community and entered the code. It was ridiculous how many people knew it. Every pizza-delivery guy, every UPS driver and gardener. Living in a gated community had been Ed's idea, probably to make him appear like an upscale citizen when, really, a person just couldn't get any lower.

Not even a hit man.

She drove down the tree-lined street, passing by homes with big porches, including the one once occupied by Ed and Justine Hays.

Goosebumps exploded on her arms. The place felt like looking at a nightmare. She never once imagined she'd return.

It's just a house. It's just a house. He can't hurt you now.

Emily made another pass in her rental car—some Nissan sedan thing—making sure no one was watching the house. By now, neighbors and the FBI had to be wondering what had happened to them.

One of them is burning in hell, thank God. Or devil? Whatever. Eventually, the mortgage company would foreclose, and the home would be sold. For the moment, however, there were no unusual-looking cars on the street. None of the lights were on inside. Everything looked quiet.

She parked several houses down on the corner.

There was a spot with several thick trees, so none of the neighbors would see her getting out. It was summertime and humid, so she'd purchased running shoes, shorts, and a tank top from the Target in El Paso on her way to the airport. She would look like a woman out for a very late-night jog.

Emily shut off the engine to her rental, removed her hoodie, put her hair up in a ponytail, and stared down the dimly lit street with her hands wrapped tightly around the steering wheel. *You can do this. No fear. That's the old you.* This time, she wouldn't let her nerves control her. Too much was at stake.

She hopped from the car and began jogging, her eyes scanning every front yard, every driveway, every tree. All clear.

Once to her old house, she ducked behind the row of overgrown bushes to the side of the yard and pushed her way through them toward the back gate.

Dismal, shameful memories flooded her mind. Ed had been incredibly sweet when they first married. He'd promised her the perfect life, starting with a big, beautiful home. When she'd seen this place, she honestly believed she was the luckiest woman in the world. A loving husband with a great job. A car all to herself. A house with big windows and a manicured lawn. It was a two-story dream, sitting atop an invisible nightmare.

Little by little, the real Ed had started crawling out from under the sick-and-twisted rock where his heart resided. Then one day, he'd shed his disguise completely. He was a monster. His lopsided, sadistic smile would haunt her to the end of time. It always brightened when she begged for mercy.

Emily had to wonder why she'd stayed so long. *What the hell was I thinking?* And in this moment, she wanted nothing more than to leave. Maybe burn the house down on her way out.

She headed through the back gate and found her spare key under the potted lemon tree by the gazebo. Ed never knew she kept it there for emergencies. He hated the idea of her losing anything. *Weak people lose shit. You lose shit.*

No. Regular people lost shit. And every once in a while, she locked herself out.

With haste, she shoved her key in the door. *This is not you. This house is not you. You are more than your past.*

She opened the back door and used the flashlight on her phone to inspect the kitchen. It had only been a few months since she'd left, but the place smelled different. Stuffy. Rotten.

Items had been moved or were missing. Just little things only she would notice. For example, the ceramic jar she kept her flour in on the counter was gone. The photos, of her and Ed on his boat, once stuck to the side of the fridge, were gone. The taupe window treatments over the breakfast nook she'd hung were gone, too. Ed had removed any trace of her.

Not a surprise, really.

She quickly checked out the rest of the house—living room, guest rooms, dining room. Everything was dusty. Strange because she would've expected Charge and his team to clean the place when they'd been here a few weeks ago. According to him, Ed had died in the bathroom upstairs. Maybe they only cleaned there?

Of course. Why'd she think they'd do the entire house?

Strange how being here didn't feel like she imagined. She wasn't even bothered knowing Ed died here. Maybe because being back didn't feel real, and this was no longer her world. It was a bad dream meant for forgetting.

Emily made her way to the den. Ed would never keep anything incriminating or valuable in an obvious place, but it wouldn't hurt to look.

She went to work, quickly inspecting underneath and inside the drawers, under his leather chair—anywhere he could've taped a key or document. All she found were their old checkbooks, which she refused to look at. She didn't want to see their names together on a piece of paper.

For good measure, she checked the pile of papers sitting in a tray on top of the desk. *Bill,*

bill, bill. Nothing, dammit.

Emily swiveled on the heel of her running shoe, the light from the streetlamp outside casting a warm yellow light through the blinds, hitting the wall just opposite.

What's that? Her flour jar sat in the middle of the bookshelf next to Ed's fishing books.

She reached up and grabbed it, placing the jar atop Ed's desk. Inside was a sealed envelope.

Why was it here?

If the FBI had been through the home, no doubt wondering what had happened to Ed, wouldn't they have taken this?

Maybe they hadn't been thorough.

Maybe they didn't suspect foul play.

She opened the letter and angled it toward the light coming through the window.

Justine,

If you're reading this, it's because you've returned home. I hope that's not the case, but if you have, leave. Go back to wherever you were and stay missing. For good. Do not attempt to contact me or anyone connected to me.

I tried to warn you in person, but you've dropped off the face of the earth. That's a good thing. It means they might not find you either.

I sure as hell hope not because they won't

hesitate hurting you to find out where I've gone, and we both know you have no spine. If they do find you, I warn you to tell them nothing. I will make you pay. You will go down with me if I'm caught.

I left money buried in the planter out back, the one where you hid your key, to help you stay gone.

Ed

What the fuck? It was dated a few days after she'd left him, well after Charge said they came to kill Ed and his team.

What was going on? Because from the sound of it, Ed had skipped town long ago.

That meant he wasn't dead!

That meant Charge lied.

And who the hell was "they"?

She shoved the letter in her pocket and braced herself on the edge of the desk. She couldn't breathe right. The coincidences had never made sense—that she ended up working for Charge, whose sister was killed by Ed. At least, that'd been Charge's story.

But what if that was a lie, too? What if Charge made it up? What if he only said all that to gain her sympathy and trust? His sister's death by Ed's hand gave them something in common. It made them both victims of the same man.

I'm so stupid. No, stupid wasn't the right

word. Overly trusting. The situation with Charge had never made sense because everything he told her was a lie. Charge probably didn't even have a sister. Because if he could lie about killing Ed, what else would he lie about?

Everything.

As for how she ended up working for Charge, maybe that was no coincidence at all. *I mean, what are the odds, right?*

But *she* had picked El Paso to hide because if worst came to worst, and Ed tracked her down, she could always go south. Still, El Paso had been *her* choice. So was answering the ad in the paper for a "we pay cash" job at a pest-control company.

So, if those were all her, was it possible this had still been a setup?

Her mind raced, her heart along with it.

Suddenly, her brain spit out the only possible explanation. Charge or someone on his team had been watching her. For months before she even split New Jersey.

All the research she did before leaving had been done at the public library on a public computer. She'd been so hyper-focused on making sure Ed didn't discover her plans to run that someone else could have been watching her. She wouldn't have noticed. They weren't Ed or one of his pervert goons—the people she'd been keeping an eye out for.

And if that someone else had been watching

her, they could've easily seen which towns she'd been researching. They would have seen her checking out bus routes to Detroit, to Chicago, then El Paso. They would have seen her hunting for cheap rentals. They would've watched her writing down directions to meet with the guy who sold fake IDs. Anyone paying attention might've easily seen her fake name on email exchanges, too.

Her blood chilled.

And if they'd known where she landed in El Paso—her old dump of a studio—who was to say they hadn't gone through her trash?

She'd made notes, starting day one of her arrival in El Paso, scribbling down names of businesses and their phone numbers for jobs she applied to—waitress, house cleaner, car wash attendant. It would have been easy for anyone to see she'd circled the "we pay cash" jobs in the local paper.

She covered her mouth with a shaky hand, feeling like she wanted to scream. It would've taken nothing for Charge to place an ad of his own. An ad she'd be likely to answer if it contained those magic words. *We pay cash.*

She always thought it was weird how she'd gotten the job so quickly. A quick chat on the phone. Done. Desperate, broke, and hungry, she'd showed up to that "pest control" office in a vacant strip mall, and everything started from there.

Idiot! Her heart felt like it was falling straight through her body, crashing to the floor. So many pieces to this entire situation hadn't fit, and she just went on telling herself it was okay. *"Just fate at work." "Charge would never hurt me." "Everything's fine."*

But if people had been after Ed, maybe gathering evidence against him and his partners, why wouldn't they have been watching her, too? They'd want to see what she knew.

So who would be after Ed?

The most obvious answer was the people who'd been watching her, who knew her every move, who manipulated her every step: Charge and his team.

She tilted her head toward the ceiling of the den, feeling like the earth was crumbling beneath her feet. *Ed is still alive.* And not just him, but his pervy brother and heartless associates, too. Had the women Ed had been trafficking gotten away? At least she hoped that part had been true.

As for the money she owed suite forty-five, she had no doubt the whole thing was a ploy to keep her in the mix—*You owe us money. You stay and work, or you die.* A calculated risk on Charge's part, but it worked.

But why keep me close?

Perhaps they hadn't expected Ed to skip town when he did. Perhaps they hoped Ed might come looking for her, giving them the opportunity to nab him. Perhaps they planned to use her as bait to bring him out of hiding?

Hell, maybe they thought she was in on Ed's business and wanted to gain her trust so she'd tip her hand.

No. Charge knows me better than that. Doesn't he? Emily ran her hands over her hair and down the back of her ponytail. For the first time since this cluster began, things were finally making sense. Except for one piece: Why go so big?

Why put on this huge, epic charade to keep tabs on her? They'd pretended to kill Ed and his team. They'd told her she was on the hook to pay them a million bucks. They'd pretended to bring her into the fold as one of them. But she knew—*knew!*—it made no sense for Charge to ask her to manage the team. And there he was, every step of the way, hurling one convincing argument after another! For every red flag she raised, he had the perfect rebuttal.

So what do they want with me?

Okay, so she didn't have all the answers surrounding their motives, but she knew enough to see the truth now. Question was, what should she do about it?

Keep playing along until she found out what they hoped to gain?

Run?

And what about Charge?

A morbid thought crept into the space of her

wounded heart: the image of Charge's battered face.

What if that part wasn't pretending? For reasons unbeknownst to her, suite forty-five had created this elaborate scheme around her, but the players on the outside were no joke. The cartels were real. She knew that. She'd watched people on Charge's team get hit by bullets and die right in front of her when they were ambushed by the cartel on the same day she was kidnapped. The abuse she took after was real, too. Also real had been Charge and the members of his team finding her just in time to execute her captors.

Real. All real.

So it wasn't completely unreasonable to assume that suite forty-five's enemies were in possession of Charge.

Emily's gut-wrenching rage for his betrayal faded into a heavy blanket, weighing down on her conscience. His lies and deceits, regardless of any underlying reasons, were unforgivable. She'd been through hell those first few weeks after meeting him, but Charge could've left her in the hands of his enemies, to live out her days drugged and raped repeatedly.

But he hadn't.

Jesus. She sighed. *How do I keep getting sucked back into all this? I'm going to save him, and then that's it. I'm done. I'm walking away.* Whatever else suite forty-five wanted from her, they weren't going to get it. She just hoped that if she managed to free Charge, he'd let her leave.

In theory, she might be saving the man who had no intention of ever letting her out of his sight.

CHAPTER TEN

"You're late," Olivia said, hopping into the car with her. Olivia had been waiting behind the gas station ten minutes longer than agreed, but Emily knew enough about the woman to understand her major peeves. Punctuality was number one. Following the rules was number two.

"Sorry about that. It took me longer than I thought to go through the house."

"Did you go in the bathroom?" Olivia asked.

"The bathroom?"

"You know, to see where it happened?"

Where Ed died. *What a messed-up thing to ask.* Especially now that Emily knew it was all a farce.

"Uh, no. I didn't. But I did go through all of Ed's hiding places."

"And?"

Emily prepared to lie. She'd decided not to let on about what she knew. Ed was alive. They were likely waiting for him to make a mistake so they could take him out. "And I found his money."

"What?"

Emily looked over her shoulder at the plastic bag she'd dug up. "Yep. It was buried in a planter."

"That must be one huge planter to hold a million dollars."

"Nope."

Olivia blinked at her. "So then, how much did you recover?"

Ignoring Olivia's question, Emily asked, "Where's Flint?"

"Across the street picking up a few guns and getting a sandwich. He said he was hungry, and his stomach waits for no one. Now answer my question. How much?"

"Picking up guns from who?" Emily asked.

Olivia gave her an impatient look. "We know people, okay? Now tell me."

This was a tricky thing to answer. She couldn't let on that she knew Ed had skipped town with his life and his money. "I think it's about one hundred thousand."

"That's all?"

"Yes."

"What about the rest?" Olivia asked.

"Who knows? I mean, I didn't find any papers, lockbox keys, anything to point us toward where he really had his money."

"How'd you find that?" She looked at the bag.

"Ed left it in the planter where I had my spare key hidden. I noticed a corner of the bag sticking out of the potting soil when I bent over to grab the key," she lied.

"Why would he leave it there?"

Emily shrugged. "Emergency cash, maybe. I don't know."

"Okay, well, I don't have to tell you it's not enough."

Emily knew that, but where could they come up with another nine hundred thousand dollars? It wasn't like she could sell her house and cash in Ed's 401(k).

"Unfortunately," Emily said, "Ed was too paranoid to leave a paper trail. The only person he really trusted was his brother." *Crap. His brother.* Why hadn't she thought about that before?

Ed had probably skipped town with Merrill, but Merrill was irresponsible and arrogant. He was a dirty cop who truly believed he could get away with anything. Likely because he always had. Which was why every time Ed told him to put "some" away for a rainy day, Merrill told him to fuck off and mind his own business.

"Ed's brother, Merrill, has a huge storage unit," Emily said. "It's one of those climate-controlled fancy places where he keeps three or four vintage Porsches, an Aston Martin, and some other cars—I don't know what they are, but he bought them at auctions. Ed always chewed him out because they're the kind of cars no cop can afford." Merrill always argued that they were investments. Not for driving. Of course, Merrill couldn't resist taking them out for a spin from time to time. But mostly, he collected them and spent his free time gleaming over his prizes, won on the backs of those poor women they trafficked.

"I'm sorry, Emily," Olivia said, "but I don't think the guys who have Charge will take cars in exchange for his life."

The back passenger door flew open, and Flint jumped in. "Hello, ladies. What are we talking about?"

"Emily just came back from her house."

"Find anything interesting?" Flint asked.

"Just one hundred thousand," Emily replied. "But we were just discussing Merrill, Ed's brother. He has a car collection probably worth well over a million dollars."

"Yeah, and like I said, that's not going to help us," Olivia spouted.

"I know of a guy." Flint popped a toothpick in his mouth. "He's not far from here—chop shop type, but he'll probably do a deal for some vintage cars."

"Really?" Emily felt a tingle of hope. "At this time of night?"

He gave her a look. "They steal cars for a living. What do you think?"

"Sorry, I haven't lived a shadier life than you," Emily fired back.

"You sure about that?" Flint replied, pushing his long hair back under his baseball cap.

"Good point." Emily's life was about as shady as it got.

Flint continued, "The unfortunate news is the guy'll probably only give you fifty cents on the dollar."

Not good. "Still, that could be five or six hundred K."

"Which leaves us with a significant deficit." Olivia looked at her watch. "And only four hours to catch our flight home to deliver the money."

Emily let out a soft groan.

"You're absolutely sure we have no hope of finding your husband's piggy bank?" Olivia asked.

"Yes." He was probably spending it right now, sipping piña coladas on some beach.

"I know a way we can make some quick money," Flint offered.

Olivia turned her entire body around to glare at him. "No."

"Yes," he replied.

"No. The last time you did a job for that man, you ended up in the hospital."

Flint shrugged. "So? I wrecked my bike."

"Running from the cops! No, Flint. I'm your partner, and I say no. Plus, there isn't enough time."

"You can deal with the cars," he argued. "Emily and I can run a job. We have plenty of time."

"What job?" Emily asked.

"Flint lived out here for a few years and knows the sort of people you don't want to get involved with," Olivia scorned.

"It's easy money. Loan shark stuff." Flint made it sound like a trip to the barber.

"What do you mean?" Emily asked.

Flint jumped in, speaking over Olivia's fervent objections. "This guy stakes high rollers, mostly down in Atlantic City, but his customers are all over. Sometimes they don't want to pay up. They need encouragement."

"No! Emily, don't do it." Olivia grabbed her arm. "They're not the type of people you need to mess around with."

There weren't a lot of options to make serious money at two o'clock in the morning. "But Charge is—"

"He's not a child," Olivia scolded. "He signed up for this gig and knew the risks. He might not want to die, but he always understood the possibilities. And he sure as hell wouldn't want you to—"

"Watch it, Olivia," Flint warned.

Olivia snapped her mouth shut.

"What? Charge wouldn't want me to what?" Emily pushed.

Olivia released a long breath. "Nothing. Never mind."

"No. Not never mind. Tell me what you were going to say, or I'm going with Flint to…to…" What did they call it in the movies? "Shake down some people."

Olivia opened her mouth, only to be silenced by Flint. "Don't do it, girl."

What did they know? What was it he didn't want Olivia to share?

"Look, guys," Emily said, "I'm not stupid, okay? I know there's way more going on than anyone's telling me. So don't think for one second that I'm not on to this clownfuckery you've all been shoving down my throat. But I believe Charge's life is really on the line, and I believe I'm alive because he saved me. So whatever's going on, I owe him one save." She held up her index finger. "Just one. And if that means I need to go scare the crap out of few stupid assholes who were dumb enough to take money from a loan shark, then so be it. *They* knew what *they* were getting into."

Flint chuckled, delighted. "You got balls, woman. I'll give you that."

"Well, let's just hope it's enough to get the money," Emily muttered. If not, Charge was dead.

CHAPTER ELEVEN

With less than four hours to go, Olivia set out to Merrill's house to locate all his car keys, titles, and any receipts with the location of the storage locker. Likely, those would be easy to find and stashed in a drawer. Then Olivia would meet up with Flint's contact to inspect the cars no one would ever miss. Merrill was on the run. Once Chop Shop Guy reached a price with Olivia, she'd hand over all the keys and paperwork and collect the money. Done. The only hurdle would be getting a reasonable deal for Merrill's collection.

As for Flint and Emily, he'd had a two-minute chummy conversation with some guy named "the Greek." Now she and Flint were already on their way to see the first late customer.

The Greek, Emily thought. *Such a cliché.* Why did guys like him always pick nicknames that sounded like they were wrestlers? The Fist. The Heavy. The Sicilian.

"So, the Greek is really going to pay us three hundred thousand dollars just to visit this one person?" Emily asked as Flint drove them in his rental through the maze of toll roads.

"Nope. He pays fifty for the visit. One hundred if the guy coughs up the money."

"How much does he owe?"

"Five hundred."

"Thousand?" Emily asked.

"Yep."

"And what if he doesn't have the money on him?"

"Trust me, he does. The Greek doesn't stake anyone who doesn't have liquidity."

"How do you know?" Emily found it hard to believe someone just had that kind of cash lying around. Okay, well, her situation was different. She'd accidentally stolen that money back home. But most people didn't have piles of cash lying around.

A call came in on her phone. It was Olivia. Emily answered and listened to the good news. Olivia had already been to Merrill's house and was on the way to meet Chop Shop Guy at the storage unit not too far from her old house.

Wow. Things were going pretty smoothly so far.

"Okay. Call us as soon as the deal's done."

Emily hung up. "All on track," she told Flint.

Flint smiled. "Olivia's incredible."

Something about the way Flint spoke gave Emily pause. Flint sounded enamored there for a second. "How long have you known her?"

"A few years. She actually brought me on board."

Really? "So you knew her before you two became partners."

"I was doing a job for the Greek and showed up to a house where she was in the middle of working, if you know what I mean. She should've taken me out, but instead she let me go."

"What did you say to convince her?"

"I asked if they had any openings and gave her my number. A few months later, she called and had me meet up with the trainer at the time for an eval."

Emily bet that Flint's looks probably helped. He was pretty cute. Nice hair, dimples, solid build. His cocky attitude left something to be desired, though. "So just like that you joined suite forty-five?"

Flint shrugged, checking the rearview mirror obsessively. "Not just like that. I'm sure they checked me out thoroughly before contacting me. Then I had to pass all their tests and train for about a year."

"Interesting." Emily tried to imagine Flint and Olivia meeting as strangers in some target's living room, the two of them armed and likely planning to shoot each other. Then they ended up as partners. Kinda funny. But maybe it was exactly like Charge'd said, Flint and Olivia were good with "fluid situations." Meant to be.

"We're almost there." Flint took a right into a residential neighborhood. "Grab that silver gun from the glovebox and put it in your..." He glanced at her outfit. She was still in shorts and running shoes. She had her hoodie tied around her waist. "Can you hide it somewhere?"

"I'll put my hoodie back on and keep it in my pocket." The hoodie had really been to keep her warm on the plane. It was way too hot outside to wear it right now, but the alternative was shoving the gun down her ass crack. She never understood why anyone would to that. Even worse was when guys shoved the gun down the front of their pants, pointed directly at their dicks. That never seemed smart.

"So," she asked, "why hasn't this guy paid the Greek?"

"Usually because the minute these gamblers have the cash in their hands, they're planning another trip to the casino to place a Hail Mary on red. The name of the game is to catch them before they blow the money. And they always do."

"How do you know so much about this?"

"I used to be one of them. I would've gambled my own mother if they'd let me."

"How'd you go from gambling addict to this profession?" Emily found it kind of interesting. Flint was young—maybe twenty-one or two. And he just said he had already been doing thug work a few years ago when he met Olivia.

"I had more gambling debt than I could pay in a lifetime, so I went to the Greek for a loan. He said no but gave me the opportunity to earn some money. Of course, I blew that cash on more gambling. He liked me—I did good work—so he offered to loan me money before I ended up in a ditch, but only if I promised never to gamble again. Pretty generous considering how much I owed, and I wasn't about to break my word. He's not known for being nice to people who piss him off or don't pay him back on time."

Oh no. "So if the client we're going to see doesn't pay, what are we expected to do?"

"Let's hope it doesn't come to that."

"Flint…" she growled.

He glanced her way. "Don't worry, I'll make you leave the room. Don't want you throwing up all over the place."

"What? No. No. No, Flint. We are *not* going to kill anyone."

"Torture. Not kill. At least for this first one. And do you want to save Charge or not?"

"Yes, but—"

"But this is what we have to do. Or you can walk away right now. Never look back. Because trust me, none of *us* will come looking for you."

"What's that supposed to mean?"

"Never mind."

"Not never mind. Tell me," she demanded, knowing she had zero leverage over Flint to make him do it. Still, she hoped he would.

"You know by now that there are things we don't say because it puts the team at risk. Then there are things that just aren't people's business to go 'round sayin'. Got it?"

"No. Don't got it."

"Well, take it up with Charge. If there's anything left of him to take."

Every step she took, she kept getting deeper into this bullshit. Worst of all, she didn't even know what this bullshit was. "If you could make this much money working for the Greek, why do you work for Sampson?"

"Nobody works for the Greek. You do a job. If you do it well, he gives you another."

"And?" Emily knew there was more to it.

"If you do a shitty job, you disappear."

That was why Olivia was so against this. She probably worried about a job going badly.

"Don't worry, sweetheart," Flint added, "if anything goes wrong, it's on me."

Emily couldn't breathe again. Flint was putting his life on the line for this. Which meant Charge was more to him than just a fellow operator. The truth of who these people really were, and who they were to each other, was still a mystery, but their loyalty and commitment went way beyond what they let on.

Case in point, neither Olivia nor Flint had complained when they found out they wouldn't be making any money coming along with her here to New Jersey. That little fuss they'd made back in El Paso about saving Charge was just another one of their mind games. Probably.

"Okay. So tell me how to make sure this all goes right."

Flint flashed another look her way. "You stay out of sight and watch my back."

"Meaning?"

"If anyone comes up on me, you put a bullet in the back of their head."

Emily's soul quaked. She hoped it wouldn't come to that. "Okay. And if we get the money from him, what next?" It was only a hundred grand. Depending on how much Olivia got for Merrill's cars, they still needed another three or four hundred thousand.

"Then we deliver the money to the Greek, and he sends us out on another job."

"At this time of night?"

"Best time to collect. People are home, tucked safely in bed. Our visit is more psychological than anything. It makes them understand the debt is real."

"You really think we can get three different

people to cough up that much money before our flight takes off?"

"No. But it's worth a try."

"Wonderful." She sighed. "I don't suppose I could convince the Greek to just loan me the money—I mean, if we fall short?"

Flint raised a dark brow. "He doesn't loan to people like you."

"Like me?"

"Broke, darlin'. They need assets, resources they can liquidate. Or in my case, skills to barter with, and before you ask, the answer is no. He won't loan me money again. It was a onetime favor."

"Oh."

"Don't worry, sweetheart, this is easy money." He paused. "The more difficult jobs are few and far between." He reached over and patted her thigh. "We'll be on that plane with more than we need."

"Are you sure?"

He chuckled. "Sure as rain in July."

Emily had no clue what that meant and didn't really care. She felt too nervous now.

She tilted her head toward the roof of the car. They'd only been in New Jersey for less than two hours, but this was already the longest night of her life.

Flint slowed down in front of a big house with a circular driveway. "We're here. You ready?"

Nope.

CHAPTER TWELVE

Honestly, shaking down people who knew they owed money to the Greek was way easier than Flint had let on. It was almost like they'd been expecting a visit.

The first guy practically threw the bag of money at Flint the moment he rang the doorbell.

No questions. No pretending why Flint was standing on his doorstep at nearly three a.m. in the morning. He simply opened the door, tossed the duffel bag to Flint's feet, apologized for not getting the money to the Greek sooner, and then slammed the door in his face.

She and Flint delivered the cash to an all-night diner in Union City, about fifteen minutes away. The cashier didn't even blink at the money. He simply pulled out the Greek's cut, handed back the duffel bag with their portion, and told Flint he'd get a text within a few minutes.

Emily had felt her insides unraveling while Flint chowed down in the car on a complimentary slice of cherry pie the cashier included. How the hell was all this so well organized? What country were they living in?

Then it dawned on her that she'd spent several years of her life with a man who'd sworn to protect the public, yet he was the biggest cockroach of them all.

The second guy they visited owed almost seven hundred thousand and took exactly thirty seconds to pay up. He'd been hanging out at an illegal poker house. How the Greek knew where to find the man, she didn't know, but she and Flint caught him smoking outside. He took one look at Flint, ran to his car, and handed over a briefcase.

What kind of moron left that kind of cash sitting in a car? She gave it some thought. Probably the kind who was stupid enough to be gambling away money he owed to the Greek. When Emily asked Flint why they received such a generous cut, he told her they were handling large sums of money, and the Greek didn't trust many people.

"Trust comes with rewards," he said. "And when you're in our field of business, it helps. I can charge a premium. But the Greek only calls me for help every blue moon when business is heavy and his regular guys can't keep up."

Apparently, just last week, Atlantic City had some big poker competition that drew all sorts of people who played side games. Greek had lots of loans to call in. Lucky her.

"Two hundred thousand dollars in two hours. Wow." Emily could hardly believe they'd made so much money, but that was their cut.

Now she and Flint were cruising down the Turnpike on their way to job three. At this rate, they'd be at the airport with almost an hour to spare. Olivia would wait for them there after she was done hocking Merrill's cars.

Easy peasy. They might actually pull this off.

"By the way, have you heard anything from Olivia?" Emily asked, wondering how much cash she'd generated.

"No."

"Wait. Hold on. She hasn't texted you with an update? Shouldn't we be worried?" Honestly, Emily would have asked sooner, but she'd been too caught up in paying visits to the Greek's customers.

Flint stayed focused on the road, tapping his thumbs to some twangy country tune on the radio.

"Hello? I asked you a question."

"I heard."

"And?" Emily pushed.

"And this is how jobs get done. We focus on completing our part."

"But what if she's in trouble? She might be sitting in a ditch somewhere right now, needing help."

Flint's posture went from laid-back to rigid. "No. Not possible."

"You don't know that, and we owe it to her to at least check." Why did Emily have to explain this to him?

"Darlin', imagine you've been paid to take out a mafia boss who is highly guarded, paranoid, and never shows his face in public. In order to pry him out of his fortress, you have to pay the maid to flush a sanitary napkin down the toilet so the plumbing backs up. Then you have to kill the plumber and pose as him so when you tell the target over the phone he won't have access to running water for three days while they replace the sewer main, your target decides to stay at his brother's home, which has ten times more security. You'll get one shot to do the job while the man leaves his compound and travels to his brother's estate, parks by the front door, and exits his vehicle. There's one tree across the street that's high enough to get a clear shot, and if you miss, not only will your target retreat into that fortress for an indefinite amount of time, but the neighbors across the street will find a man on their doorstep offering the equivalent of five thousand dollars to chop down their tree."

"Okay."

"Do you see all the moving parts?" Flint raised a concerned eyebrow.

"Yes."

"So if the maid is worrying about climbing a tree to take the shot, how does that help anyone?"

What Flint meant was that everyone had to do their job and focus on execution; otherwise, no one else could do their part. "What did he do?"

"Who?" Flint asked.

"The guy you're hypothetically trying to kill."

"What's that got to do with anything?" he snapped.

"Everything. The team'll fight harder to make the job a success if they believe in it."

"That's not the damned point, Emily."

"I think it is. I think it's also about trust and each person in the chain of events knowing that the team has their back. If you abandon Olivia, she might live, but she will never trust you again because she's witnessed your actions firsthand. And so will I. Which means I will always be thinking in the back of my head I can't trust you. You won't have my back when things go wrong."

"Everyone on the team knows the rules. They know what they signed up for. The job comes first."

"Sounds like a stupid rule," Emily muttered, crossing her arms over her chest. "But thank God for Sampson and his rules, so you and your tiny brain know what to do. Idiot," she muttered.

"What did you say?" he growled.

"Nothing." Emily couldn't help mouthing off. She was mad.

"You realize what I do for a living, yes?" Flint threw back.

"You follow rules and pretend like you don't care about anyone, including your partner, when anyone can see that you do."

Flint grumbled something unintelligible. "Fine. Call her. We'll go from there."

"Thought you'd see it my way." Emily called Olivia, but it went straight to voicemail. She looked at Flint, that worried churning in her stomach turning into something far worse. "No answer."

"Try again."

Emily did. Same result.

Flint stared ahead at the road for a long moment. "Sonofabitch." He veered onto the off-ramp. "You're a real pain in my ass, Emily. You know that?"

She didn't respond. Because it didn't matter what he thought of her. If Olivia was in trouble, then they were all in trouble. Even Charge.

Emily looked at her watch as she and Flint pulled up to the curb one block from the storage facility where Merrill had his cars stored. Olivia had come here to meet Chop Shop Guy—a man Flint didn't really know personally. He was a "good friend" of a "good friend," and neither were answering Flint's calls.

If the cold sweat down Emily's back was right, something had gone wrong. And from the enraged look on Flint's red face, he agreed.

"You wait here." Flint checked his gun. "Get behind the wheel and keep the engine running and the doors locked."

"What do you think happened to her?" Emily asked.

"Hell if I know." Flint hopped out. "Keep your gun close but out of sight."

He shut the door, and she slid behind the wheel. Her heart was thumping so hard she felt like there were drums inside her ears. Five minutes passed, and Flint came walking down the sidewalk away from the storage complex. No Olivia.

Emily popped the lock, and he hopped in the passenger seat, shutting the door behind him.

"Well?" Emily couldn't read the look on his face.

"The security guard says she left with two guys."

"Did she leave on her own, or did they take her?" Emily's voice trembled with fear.

"What do you think?" he snarled and then muttered, "I'll kill the sonofabitches if they touch her."

Emily stared at Flint, a light bulb coming on. "Are you in love with her?"

He turned his head, nostrils flaring and an ice-cold look in his eyes.

"Sorry. It's none of my business."

"Let's move."

Emily realized she had to watch herself. Flint was in killer mode. Almost a completely different person, really. No charming, cocky smiles. No "darlin's." Just all business.

"Yes. Sorry." Emily put the car in drive. "Where do we find these guys?"

"Head back the way we came. Their shop is about twenty minutes west of the airport."

Well, at least they might still catch the flight. Only problem was, they were shy one hit woman and about seven hundred thousand dollars.

Emily made a U-turn in the middle of the street. "What are we going to do when we get there?"

Flint was silent for a long moment, raising her stress level to a full-blown ten. She had no idea what he planned to do next, and from everything she'd learned, Flint could be reckless. Emily just hoped he was keeping Olivia's safety in mind. This wasn't the time for macho revenge. Getting her back was the priority.

Emily glanced over at him in the passenger seat. His chest was rising and falling quickly. His face was red with rage. "Flint? What's the plan?"

"We're going to kill them."

Emily's stomach rolled. "Of course we are." What else would Flint do to a person who touched his woman?

CHAPTER THIRTEEN

Chop Shop Guy turned out to be the owner of a chain of exotic auto part stores in the Short Hills neighborhood. Petri's Auto Parts, for European cars and collectors.

Well, well. So Mr. Petri was a thug who apparently decided to make his own supply chain of merchandise. How interesting.

"Are you sure they're here?" Emily asked as they pulled into the parking lot.

"I'm sure they're not."

"Then why are we here?"

"Because his private garage is a few minutes down the road. Come on." Flint exited the car and grabbed a tire iron from the trunk. She followed him, wondering what the hell he was up to. Unfortunately, Flint wasn't in a talking mood, and she wasn't about to poke the assassin-bear.

They went around to the back of the building

to a large bay door. Next to that was a regular door. Probably the employee entrance.

Flint took the tire iron and did something she'd never seen before. He wedged it between the doorjamb and the handle and then pried. The door handle broke clean off, leaving a hole and access to the door's mechanism. He pushed his finger inside, jiggled something, and the door popped open.

"Wow. Remind me not to ever spend money on a lock again. Total waste of time."

"Come on." Flint entered the building first, turning on the lights.

Emily let out a slow breath to steady her nerves, and then followed him inside. It was a fairly messy garage with an attached office that had a big window looking out over the room. An old green car sat up on cement blocks in the middle of the oil-stained concrete floor. The hood was open, the engine missing, and parts were laid out on a dirty plastic table in front of it.

"Now what?" she asked.

"We wait." Flint tossed the table on its side, sending parts crashing to the floor. Nuts and bolts went everywhere.

But where was Olivia? How was this plan going to get her back? "We don't have time to sit around and—"

"I just tripped the silent alarm."

"We're waiting for the cops?" Was Flint completely nuts?

Flint's brows furrowed. "You think guys like these want the police poking around? They handle their own security."

"Oh. Oh shit." Emily patted her hoodie pocket, making sure she hadn't forgotten her gun. Petri or one of his guys was going to show up to check out whoever'd broken in. "What do we do when he gets here?"

"We get him to talk. Get the lay of the land."

Flint might come off as reckless, but he wasn't. The guy was a fast thinker. He probably figured going into the other garage with guns blazing wasn't the best idea. Maybe they had men with guns. Maybe a lot of men. He wanted to know what he was dealing with before figuring out how to get Olivia back.

Smart.

They crouched down behind the table and waited. Just like Flint said, a car pulled up outside the back door. She heard men's voices. Two, maybe three. One said he'd go around front. The other said he'd check things out back here.

Flint held up his hand, urging Emily to stay put while footsteps approached.

"Come out, and I'll consider only breaking your arms," the man said.

Flint stayed down, his gun in hand. Emily felt like she might actually wet herself, even though she held a gun, too. She had no clue what Flint was going to do.

Flint sprang up and fired off a round.

Emily felt like her eardrum had been smacked with a baseball bat. She pressed one hand to her ear, trying to stop the ringing. Slowly, she stood.

Mistake. Right next to the gutted car, a man lay on his back, a hole in his forehead.

Oh God. She turned away and shut her eyes. "Why'd you kill him?"

"I missed. I meant to hit his shoulder."

Still facing away from Flint, she opened her eyes, spotting the barrel of a gun poking out from the doorway leading to the front of the building.

The other man.

It was a reaction, pure survival instinct, but before she knew what she was doing, her hand fired. She hit the guy's wrist, and his gun tumbled to the floor.

I don't believe it. She was usually a terrible shot.

Flint didn't waste any time getting over to the guy and kicking the gun away.

"Where is she?" Flint snarled.

"Who, man?" the guy groaned in agony. Emily couldn't see him from where she stood—he'd fallen back—but she didn't need to.

"The blonde selling those cars tonight. Where'd you take her?" Flint asked.

"Nowhere, man. She said there were more cars in another storage unit across town. They went to check 'em out."

"Then why isn't she answering her phone?" Flint snarled.

"I don't know. Maybe her battery died." The guy moaned between sentences. "But she's with Mikey right now. I swear. Call him on my phone."

Olivia was Miss Cautious and Careful. It seemed out of character to let her phone die and not find another way to check in.

Emily walked over, staring down at the bald man with a tat-covered neck, cradling his bleeding wrist.

"Hand over the phone," she said.

"It's in my back pocket." Neck Tats rolled to the side, and she plucked it out of his jeans pocket.

"Passcode?" Emily asked.

"One, one, two, two."

How creative.

"What are you doing?" Flint kept his gun pointed at Neck Tats.

"He's lying. Olivia never said anything about going to a second garage." Emily found the last text messages on the guy's phone from someone named "boss." It said something about making sure to hurry up. He needed help moving the cars before "her friend comes looking" and the security guard's shift ended.

So they'd paid off that guard at the storage

unit to look the other way? *I swear, if there's enough time, I'm going back there to remove his pinky toe!*

Emily started texting while she spoke. *"With her friends now. They're offering interesting information in exchange to get her back."* Emily waited a moment.

"Anything?" Flint asked.

"No." She shook her head.

Flint turned his anger toward Neck Tats on the floor, pointing his gun right at his balls. "Where the fuck is she? I'll give you three seconds to answer."

"I don't know! They tied her up and threw her in the car!"

Emily noted how fast Flint's method worked. *Take gun; point at dick.* She filed it away for future use.

"Why? What do they want?" Flint asked.

The man didn't answer.

Emily kicked him in the ribs. "He asked a question, you turd."

Flint's brown eyes widened with shock. Emily shrugged.

Neck Tats curled up in a ball, whimpering. "Petri didn't like her price, okay?"

So basically, they showed up and wanted the cars but didn't want to pay whatever Olivia was asking. And instead of negotiating with her, they threw her in the back of their car.

"Does Petri have any clue who you are?" Emily asked Flint.

"I guess not."

That explained why Petri would even attempt to mess with Flint. He probably figured that Flint was just some lowlife looking to make a quick buck.

Emily crouched down and hit the call "boss" button on the man's cell.

"What?" Petri's scratchy voice came over the phone. He sounded older. Definitely jaded.

"Hi," Emily said sweetly, "I'm here in your lovely store filled with really wonderful stolen car parts."

"Who the fuck is this?" Petri growled.

Flint frowned at her, almost looking curious but not objecting to whatever her plan was. It felt nice to be trusted, she thought.

"Wrong question, Mr. Petri," Emily said. "What you should be asking is who is Flint. Or, more accurately stated, who does he work for? I'll give you a hint: His boss runs a group of hired guns out of Texas. I doubt you've heard of him, because Texas is pretty far from your little circle of criminals, but I will tell you this interesting piece of information. That woman you're holding also works for the same man. And he doesn't take it kindly when idiots like you fuck with his people."

The man laughed. "Nice try. I admire your

balls, lady. But Petri don't run from nobody."

Emily smiled. "Who said I was asking you to run? I'm asking you to get your ass over here and drop off our wonderful friend along with five hundred thousand dollars for the cars you planned to steal from under our noses. In exchange, you won't end up with a forehead makeover." Emily walked over to the dead man next to the gutted car. She snapped off a pic and texted it to Petri. "Flint really has excellent aim, wouldn't you say?"

"Wha-wha—you killed him?" Petri's raspy voice was all shock.

"No. Not me," she said innocently. "I only shot your other guy in the wrist. He's in a lot of pain, but I'm, like, ninety-nine percent sure he'll live if you get him to a hospital within the next hour."

"I'll kill you. I'll fucking kill you," Petri snarled.

"No. You'll take a breath, shove that giant ego up your ass, and think about how much you have to lose. At the moment, you're getting well over a million dollars' worth of pristine collectable cars for the bargain price of six hundred thousand."

"You said five."

"Did I? Oops. It's six now. And not only will you be getting a sweet deal on cars no one will ever come looking for, but you'll get to keep your shop, your life, and one of the men you sent here to kill us."

The other end of the line went silent, but she knew he was still there. Probably muted them.

She put the phone on mute too and looked at Flint. "Should I have asked for more? Six hundred still puts us shy, but maybe we still have time to do the last job for the Greek."

"The Greek! You're working for the Greek?" Petri's voice came over the cell.

Oh shit. She thought she'd hit the mute button. Obviously, she hadn't. She'd been using mostly burner phones lately, and this guy had a new Android she'd never seen before.

Flint stayed calm and jumped right in, like a pro. "Yeah, I do favors for the Greek."

"Look, you tell him to give me another two days, and I'll give you back your friend here."

So Petri owed the Greek? *Wow. Wow. Wow. Small world.* And Petri thought he'd steal the cars and do whatever to Olivia so he didn't have to pay up. *What a dirty asshole.*

"What about the money?" Emily asked Petri.

"I can do five, but that's it. I'm already in the hole to the Greek."

"No," Emily said firmly, "we'll get you the extra two days. You give us our friend and the six. Otherwise, we tell our boss you took one of his very nice operators, *and* we tell the Greek that you had the money you owed, but you spent it all at the casino."

Flint gave Emily a look. "Put it on mute," he whispered.

"One sec, Mr. Petri." Emily hit the mute button, double-checking to make sure she did it correctly this time. "What?"

"Ask him if he lives on Oakdale Street. In the yellow house. Wife. Two teenaged kids. A cocker spaniel."

"Why?"

"Just do it," Flint demanded.

Emily drew a breath, unmuted, and asked.

"How-how do you know that?" Petri shuddered.

This time, Flint didn't hold back. "Because you're next on my hit list tonight, you fuck. So bring our friend here now, or our next stop will be your house."

Really? Petri was their third stop? It really was a small world.

Emily saw the opportunity materializing before her eyes. Petri owed the Greek but was shy money. Otherwise, he wouldn't have tried to steal the cars instead of paying. They needed seven hundred thousand to complete the million. If Petri were given more time, he could probably sell those cars for a lot more. Merrill had put a lot of money into his collection over the years.

"New deal," Emily said. "We'll talk to the Greek and get you seven days. But we want Olivia here in ten minutes. And we want seven."

"Seven!" Petri roared.

"What's your life worth, Mr. Petri? How about your family? Because you know the Greek didn't put you on Flint's list just for fun, and I know what I'd do if it were my family's lives on the line."

Everything. She'd do everything. But with her dad and aunt gone, she didn't have anyone.

Maybe this group of hit men filled that void, and that was why she'd been so quick to believe Charge and his lies. If he'd been watching her, researching her, it wouldn't have been hard for him to figure that out.

After all, she'd married Ed. She'd been to the hospital several times over the twelve-month period before she finally left him. Concussion, fractured arm, stitches on her nose that left a lovely scar. No woman in her right mind would take that kind of abuse if she wasn't terrified or brainwashed to believe she had no other choice.

And it wasn't beyond crazy to conclude that Charge knew what a mess she was because he had a basic understanding of human psychology. Understanding people and their behavior was invaluable in this line of work. Her own empathy, at least to some extent, had managed to keep her alive while doing time at prison-Ed. She'd learned what made him tick, what made him less likely to punch; she became a student of all things to avoid his rage.

Until one day, she saw herself in the mirror. She saw what would happen to those women in that lonely, violent house where they were kept. It had been a wake-up call.

"Look, Mr. Petri," she said, doing her best to sound as genuine as she felt. "One person is already dead. How many more do you want tonight? Because the way I see it, we're in a position to help each other. Or not. It's up to you, but either way, Flint and I aren't leaving without our friend. And the Greek isn't going to let you off without paying him. I'm offering you a fair deal."

Silence fell again, but she could hear Petri breathing.

"We'll be outside in ten." The line went dead.

Emily looked at Flint. "You think he'll pull anything?"

"We're about to find out."

CHAPTER FOURTEEN

An hour later, Olivia was safe and sound and boarding the plane with Emily. They sat separately, both carrying a duffel bag. Five hundred thousand dollars in each. A miracle. They'd done it. If this were any other occasion, Emily would be ordering champagne. Or tequila. Anything with alcohol, really, but she was too fried to even think.

That crap-fest back there had left her with an adrenaline hangover like no other. But Petri had seen the light and kept his word. The Greek agreed to give him more time because Flint said he'd stay a few extra days and clean up some other tabs for free. Everyone was happy.

An hour into the flight, Olivia came over. "Hey, can I sit here?" Olivia asked the woman next to Emily in the aisle seat. "My sister and I just lost our grandmother and could use a few moments."

The woman in her fifties not only vacated the seat but hugged Olivia on her way out.

Olivia plunked down next to Emily.

"We shouldn't be seen together, and it's not nice to lie like that," Emily said flatly, finally starting to feel the sting of suite forty-five's betrayal. She felt gullible for buying all their BS. Especially because she'd risked her life to save Olivia just now. And Charge, too.

"I'm in a rule-breaking mood, for once. And lies are a necessary part of the trade," Olivia threw back.

Emily occupied herself with the in-flight TV. She didn't want to talk. Or debate. Not with this woman.

"You seem like you're still processing what just happened," Olivia patted Emily's hand on the armrest, "but I just wanted to say thank you for sticking your neck out. Flint told me what you did."

"Stop." Emily jerked her hand away. "Stop blowing smoke up my ass."

Olivia furrowed her blonde brows. "I'm trying to say thank you."

Emily leaned in close and whispered, "You can say thank you by being honest. I know Ed is still alive. I know Charge lied about the million dollars I was on the hook for. The only thing I don't know is why. Why put me through all that if you could've just tied me to a chair for thirty minutes and put a few bamboo shoots up my fingernails to find out if I had anything to do with Ed's side business."

"A half an hour is a little optimistic."

Emily glared. "Fuck you."

"I'm sorry." Olivia held up her palms. "I was only trying to lighten the mood."

"You think I need a lighter mood after I saved you and put my ass on the line for Charge, after knowing what you've all done?"

Olivia sighed and looked away.

"All I want to know is why. Why do this to me?"

"You'd have to ask Charge that," Olivia finally replied.

"You really don't know?"

"When Charge tells us to do something, we do it. We don't ask for reasons. He's Sampson's right hand."

So this entire charade was all Charge? "Son-ofabitch," Emily muttered underneath her breath.

"Emily, I have no right to ask this, but please hear him out before you decide."

"Decide what?" she snarled.

"If you let him live."

"Live?" Emily raised both brows.

"Well, you're the one who has to broker the deal with Dearheart."

"You think I'm going to walk away with all that money and leave him to die? After he saved me?"

"No?"

"I'm not an immoral, lying asshole like the rest of you. I would never do that. But I might put a bullet in his head after he's safe."

"Well," Olivia patted Emily's thigh, "glad to hear it. But then please listen to his reasoning before you put a bullet in his head."

"Why the hell would I do that, knowing all of you have lied, manipulated, and made fun of me behind my back?"

"And you haven't lied, Emily Rockford? Or is it Emily Wilson this week?"

"That's not the same thing. I lied to save my life."

She shrugged. "We all have our reasons, but for the record, no one ever made fun of you. And while I don't know why Charge decided to test you like he has, I do know he always has his reasons."

"Good for him."

"He's never, and I mean never, put so much attention into anyone," Olivia added.

"And?"

"And it means something." Olivia shifted in her seat to face Emily dead on. "Charge isn't like anyone you'll ever meet. Not in a million years. He fears nothing. He'll throw himself on a grenade for you. But he never lets anyone in." She stared for a long moment with her green eyes.

"Just you."

Emily scoffed. Charge had lied to her. Repeatedly. How was that "letting her in"?

Olivia started massaging her wrists. She had rope burns. The image was a reminder of how far Emily'd come in such a short time.

"Sorry. But I'm done being played," Emily said, feeling proud of her new backbone.

"Not all plays are based on malfeasance, Emily. Sometimes they're simply good intentions, masked to keep others from seeing the truth."

"What the hell are you talking about?"

Olivia looked uncomfortable all of a sudden. "Nothing. Never mind. Just know, you have my respect and always will. Not many people will go out of their way to save the life of an assassin."

"Does that mean you and everyone else will stop lying to me?" Emily asked.

"I'll see what I can do."

"Not much of a consolation prize."

"I know. But getting an all-access pass to a team like ours takes time. And trust."

Emily raised a brow. She'd proven from the beginning she could be trusted.

Olivia went on, "Like I said, I'll see what I can do, but you have to be patient. Suite forty-five isn't what you think. We're...family."

"A family who kills together stays together?" Emily chuckled bitterly, feeling like Olivia was selling her another lie. Did Olivia really think she was so needy and pathetic that she'd buy this story and then do anything to be a part of their little "family"?

Whatever this game was, Emily didn't know. She'd probably have to torture Charge to get answers, like Olivia said.

But first things first.

The moment they landed, Emily turned on her phone and dialed Dearheart. "It's Emily. I have what you've asked for."

"Has your team vacated the border as agreed?"

Emily put the phone on mute and looked at Olivia, who was still sitting beside her, waiting for the plane to clear out. "Has the team left town?"

"As far as I know."

Emily unmuted the phone. "They're gone. It's just me and another teammate."

"I said everyone had to be out."

"Well, I need help carrying all this stuff, so you'll just have to make an exception."

"Is it Olivia?" he asked.

How did Dearheart know her name? Oh yes, he'd IDed at least ten members of their hit-tribe.

"Yes," Emily replied.

"That's fine. She's a handler."

Handler? So was that her official role? She "handled" Flint? Interesting.

He added, "See you at the Rusty Nail. Noon."

Noon gave her a little extra time. "See you then."

Emily ended the call and looked at Olivia. "I have a bad feeling about this."

"Good. That feeling generally comes in handy when you're dealing with people like him."

"Nice to know." But that wasn't at all what Emily was referring to. Something about this entire situation just felt...off.

If this rival group wanted the border territory, why not just pick off suite forty-five one by one, starting with Charge? Why give him back? Yes, two million was a lot of money, but weren't they worried that Charge (aka Sampson) would bring everyone back the moment he was free?

And what about revenge? Charge wasn't going to be too happy about getting the shit kicked out of him.

Emily looked at Olivia, who was just about to stand and exit the plane. "Are you sure this isn't another test?"

"You mean Charge being taken?" Olivia rolled her eyes. "No. Look what we've been through in the last twenty-four hours." She lowered her voice. "You even shot someone."

Olivia seemed to be telling the truth. And honestly, Emily knew that the man Flint shot had genuinely died. That hadn't been fake blood. "Are you telling me everything you know about these people?"

"I know nothing about them other than they used to control the border. Sampson ran them out years ago. Why?"

"I feel like we're walking into a trap or something. I mean, if you were them, why would *you* let us live? Why hand over Charge?"

Olivia mulled for a moment and sat back down, whispering, "I probably shouldn't tell you this, but we all have backers."

Backers. "What kind of backers?"

"You don't really think our work goes unnoticed? Who do you think helps us cover up investigations? How do you think we get half the information on the targets?"

"So like, CIA? FBI? What?" Emily whispered back.

"I can't tell you anything more right now. Just trust me when I say there would be some very upset people in high places if we were picked off."

"And if Charge were killed?"

"They only care about jobs getting done. So if a death doesn't interrupt the work flow, then probably not. People come and go—mostly go—in this profession. A few losses are expected."

For the first time, Emily finally felt like she was getting a straight answer. No, Olivia hadn't told her everything, but reading between the lines, Emily understood that their group wasn't operating in a vacuum. "Does this rival team have backers, too?"

Olivia stood. The plane was empty, and the flight attendant was coming over to shoo them out. "Everyone answers to someone."

Okay. Interesting. Emily got up and followed Olivia out, her mind working overtime. This idea of backers put a whole new dangerous perspective on things. For the first time in her life, she answered to no one. Not Ed—wherever that fucker was—not Charge, and certainly not these backers.

So who were they, these backers? What sort of people ordered hits?

Bad people?

Powerful people?

Rich people?

Whatever the answer, Emily wanted nothing to do with this kind of stuff. She thought suite forty-five was hired by people who needed help. This was different. And it was time to run.

I'm getting Charge freed, and then I'm out.

CHAPTER FIFTEEN

With fifty minutes to spare, Emily checked into a cheap motel near the airport so she could shower off yesterday's sweat and change into yet another bargain-bin outfit, this one coming from the drugstore next door. She knew she'd look pretty ridiculous in orange boardshorts, a *Don't Mess With Texas* T-shirt, and Lone Star State flip-flops, but she was not about to show up to meet Dearheart in running shorts, smelling like she'd actually run a marathon, which was how last night felt.

Next she'd swing by the gallery on the way and grab her belongings along with the money in the vault. Once Charge was free, she'd head straight out of town on the first bus to anywhere. Then she'd find another cheap motel and sleep for a week before deciding where to go next. At least she still had the ten grand Charge had given her sitting in the bank. It wasn't enough to live off of, but it was enough to get her away from El Paso.

Emily showered, dressed, downed an iced espresso in a can from the vending machine, and then hopped in an Uber to the gallery. She had just enough time to collect the rest of the money and get to the Rusty Nail, but her stomach and nerves were amping up. Facing Dearheart again wasn't something she looked forward to, and more importantly, this situation still felt off. Very off.

Yeah, you're an idiot for doing this. That's what's off. But she owed Charge this one thing. Then they were square.

Her ride dropped her in front of the gallery. She lugged her bags filled with money to the door and dug her keys from her purse. The moment she shoved the key into the front door, it swung open. The lock was busted.

Oh no. Her blood pressure dropped. She took a small step inside the empty space, looking and listening. All was quiet. And, honestly, there wasn't much to steal—some mugs, a temperamental espresso machine, and her clothes in the back room. It wasn't like she had a gold mine…

Her knees went weak. She ran to the supply closet, where the entrance to the walk-in safe was.

The door was open. The safe was empty.

"No. No, no, no!" She ran inside the safe and spun on her heel. *How did this happen?* Once she'd taken over the lease, she personally saw to it that the combination had been changed.

Her mind shuffled, remembering the day two locksmiths had showed up to help her reset the combination. One laughed and commented that a high school student with access to YouTube could hack it.

Okay, but still, how the hell did anyone even know the money was there? She'd only told Charge, Olivia, and Flint.

Charge was tied up, Flint was in New Jersey paying back that favor, and…

Olivia. Fucking Olivia! There was no one else who could have done this. *But why?* Why would she take the money needed to free Charge?

Oh my God. I'm going to be sick. What was she going to do now? She had less than twenty minutes to meet Dearheart.

Okay. Okay. Don't panic. She could still make this work, right? Deliver one million to Dearheart with a side dish of fake bills? If she were lucky, she'd have Charge free before they realized only half the money was there.

"I can do this. I can do this." She whooshed out a breath. "I can definitely do this." Emily grabbed the bags of money and reached for the door. "No I can't."

Dearheart wasn't an idiot. He would check to be sure all the money was there before letting Charge go, wouldn't he?

Emily looked at her watch. She might still have time to reason with Olivia.

Emily grabbed her cell and dialed, but it went straight to Olivia's voicemail. If there was any hope of getting the money back, Emily'd have to go in person, but she had no clue where Olivia lived.

Think. Think. Think.

Emily called Flint, who picked up right away, sounding groggy. "What?"

"Hey, it's Emily. I don't want to alarm you, but I think something's up with Olivia," she lied. "She's not answering her phone, and she was supposed to meet me here at the gallery before we head over to the Rusty Nail."

Silence.

"Flint?" Emily prodded.

"Yeah, I'm here." He sounded angry. "I knew I shouldn't have stayed behind. Sonofabitch!"

"Where does she live? I have time to go to her place before I'm supposed to meet Dearheart, but only if I hurry."

"She's renting a house. Two eleven West Mariposa."

"Okay. Got it."

"Emily, listen to me. If she's in trouble—"

Emily hung up, uninterested in anything more Flint had to say.

She searched the address on her phone.

Okay. Olivia's is eight minutes away. This was

doable if Olivia was still there. Either way, Emily's choices were now showing up with only half the money or showing up a little late, hopefully with all the money. The latter was better.

Emily entered the address in her ride app. *One minute away! Yes!* She hit "confirm" and went to stand outside the gallery with her duffel bags.

All she could do now was hope that Olivia hadn't split town yet. Emily had no clue why Olivia would betray her like this, but maybe there was a good reason. A reason she could work through.

Emily had no choice but to leave one million dollars in cash in the trunk of a car belonging to a complete stranger. Her only rationale for this was that if for some reason the Uber driver took off with her stuff, he wasn't completely untraceable.

"I'll be right back, okay?" Emily said to the driver.

"Sure. No problem."

"Good. Because I plan to give you a hundred bucks' tip if you get me to my next appointment on time. I can't miss my meeting." The next stop was the Rusty Nail.

She hopped out and walked up to the small, mint green house with white shutters. Emily entered without knocking. No time. "Olivia!

Hello?"

The living room was free of any personal items. The furniture—an Ikea couch, a few bookshelves, and some framed photos of flowers on the wall—looked like the stuff belonging to this rental. Nothing belonging to Olivia.

Had she already left? "Olivia, if you're still here, come out. I just want to talk, okay? If you need money, I'm sure we can figure out a way to get you some. Flint, me, Charge. We'll do whatever it takes, but Charge is going to lose his life if that money isn't handed over."

Emily held her breath, praying to God that the house wasn't empty.

A muted sob thrummed through the wall.

"Olivia?" Emily followed the noise past the all-yellow bathroom to a bedroom door.

Emily knocked. "Hey, talk to me. What's going on?"

The sobs grew louder.

"Olivia?" Emily turned the handle and entered, finding a mess of puffy green eyes, hiccups, and a few suitcases next to the bed.

"I'm sorry." Olivia bawled into her hands.

Emily sat down next to her on the bright floral comforter, patting her back. "Why did you steal the money?"

"I'm pregnant. And after last night, I know I can't do this anymore. I can't raise a kid like this."

Oh boy. Now Emily understood. The money

wasn't a greed move. It was a survival, protective-mother-to-be move.

"But you can't tell anyone." Olivia sniffled. "No one can know. Not even Flint. He's reckless, Emily. He's dangerous. What kind of father would that make, huh?"

The baby was Flint's? *I knew something was going on between those two.* And, unfortunately, there was a strict no-getting-frisky-with-teammates rule.

Emily slowly exhaled. "I am not going to even try to give you or him advice, because I have no idea what this suite forty-five thing really is. But I can tell you this, Olivia: Flint almost lost his mind when Petri took you. Does that mean he loves you? I don't know. But I've been with a man who didn't want the best for me. If someone had taken me, he wouldn't have lifted a finger to get me back. So, given Flint's actions to protect you, you at least owe him one shot. Just one. He might step up and choose an exit strategy for the three of you. If he doesn't, then you know. But at the very least I think you should give him a chance. That is, if you want him in your life." Emily sighed. "Of course, I barely know him. So if he's crazy as fuck, then trust your instincts and run. Your child comes first."

Olivia chuckled bitterly under her breath. "How'd you do that?"

"What?"

"Make it all sound so simple?"

"Maybe because it is, once you sift through the BS."

Olivia bobbed her head of messy blonde hair.

"I'm sorry to rush you, but my ride is waiting outside, and I have to get to the Rusty Nail before Charge becomes man-sashimi."

"The money's in the closet."

Emily sprang up from the bed and jerked open the closet door. Really? Olivia had shoved all the money into one extra-large suitcase. No wheels. "I can't carry all the money alone."

"Sorry. I switched everything out. Just in case there were trackers."

Why didn't I think of that? "Can you help me get this to the bar?"

"Yeah." Olivia rubbed her tears away and stood. "Why are you so nice to me?"

"What do you mean?" In her mind, she hadn't been anything.

"I took money from you. Money you need to save the man you love. How are you not putting a bullet in my head right now?"

Emily frowned. "A, I do not love Charge. B, you just told me you're pregnant." She reached out and squeezed Olivia's arm. "Why in the world would I hurt you for just trying to make a better life for you and your baby?"

Olivia sighed. "I swear, Emily, you're from another goddamned planet."

Emily nodded. "Probably. But can we figure out which one after we have Charge back?"

"Sure. Whatever you say, boss."

"Funny." Emily pointed to Olivia's phone. "You might want to tell Flint you're okay before he has a cardiac."

"Nah. I think he needs a little reality check. It might give him clarity when I break the news and give him the choice."

Stay a hit man or be with Olivia and start fresh.

Emily knew which one she'd choose if she were him. Love. Family. The absence of the two in her life, ever since her dad and Aunt Mary died, felt like a massive void. It was hard to admit it, but so many of her wrong choices in life were in response to that—trying to regain what she'd lost.

"All right," Emily said, "let's get moving." She looked at the time. *Oh God. Five minutes.* They were going to be late. "You have a gun, right?"

"Yes. Why?"

"I'm still worried something's seriously up with this deal." She knew what Olivia'd said, about the various backers, but this act of war wasn't making sense. Take Charge, ask for money, demand suite forty-five leave the border area. That couldn't be their entire plan.

"Then trust your instincts, but I can't stay and back you up." She slid her hand over her stomach.

In other words, Emily was on her own to do

this deal. She felt the sweat accumulating down her back. But there was no other choice. If she walked away now, she could never live with herself.

"Emily?" Olivia frowned and looked her over. "What the hell are you wearing?"

CHAPTER SIXTEEN

Olivia drove Emily in her old blue pickup to the shady bar that was fast becoming Emily's least favorite place on the planet. Every time she came to the Rusty Nail, something terrifying happened.

They parked in the alley behind the bar, and she and Olivia unloaded the bags, carrying them inside through the back door to the table in the corner.

Like usual, there were only a few patrons. The bartender was busy unpacking cases of alcohol and showed zero interest in what they were doing. It was almost like he was paid not to pay attention. Maybe he was.

"Okay. You're all set." Olivia dragged over the large suitcase. "Next time make sure to only steal hundreds. Much more manageable." Some of the cash from the cartel had been twenties.

Emily laughed. The notion that she'd ever

touch this much money again was hysterical. Two million dollars. Enough money for her to live on, modestly and comfortably, forever.

"So what are you going to do?" Emily asked.

Olivia shrugged. "First, I'm going to call Flint. Then I'm getting out of town. With or without him."

"What will you do for money?"

"I have enough saved up to last a little while. Maybe a year if I really stretch it. After that, I'll just have to see."

Emily guessed that if Flint joined Olivia, things would be easier. He had his own rainy-day fund. There'd been a mention of an Italian winery, too. Sounded nice. "I wish I could do something for you."

"You've been a friend." Olivia smiled warmly. "And trust me, I haven't had one of those in a very long time."

"What about Flint?" Emily asked.

"He doesn't count. Friends don't let friends get knocked up. Or do the knocking. Not my friends, anyway." Olivia handed her the gun. "A parting gift."

"Wow. I feel so loved." Emily chuckled.

"I'd better get going. Dearheart's probably out front, wondering where you are." Olivia headed for the back exit. "Good luck."

"You, too." Emily watched her leave, trying not to get caught up in the fear of being all alone to see this through. If anything went wrong, she was dead. Charge was dead. No one would be coming to rescue them.

Before she could allow those thoughts to fully settle, the front door opened. In walked Dearheart in a black suit.

"There you are." His dark eyes swept up and down her body. "You going to the beach?"

Yes, yes. She still had on her very strange board shorts, tourist tee, and flip-flops. "Nope. Meeting with you is all the sunshine I need."

Dearheart walked straight for her and stopped. "Is it all there?" He eyed the bags of money.

"Yes."

"And everyone's out of town. For good?" he added.

"Yes."

"Then let's get this done." He went for one of the bags.

Emily stepped in front of him, blocking his way. "I want to see Charge first."

"He's right outside. You'll see him."

"I want to see him now," she insisted. "Then you can have your money."

Dearheart narrowed his eyes and held out his hand, gesturing toward the door. "If you like."

Clearly, the guy didn't fear her or any deceptions she might bring to the table. Instantly, Emily started to wonder if this was just another of

Charge's elaborate tests. It didn't feel right that the man was so relaxed while her insides felt like windmills on a gusty day.

She stepped outside, her eyes scanning the nearly empty parking lot. A few cars were parked in front of the old pizzeria. A white van sat alone in the middle of the lot, parked diagonally across several places.

"He's in there." Dearheart pointed to the van.

Emily wanted to be cautious. She wanted to play her cards right, but knowing Charge was inside, waiting to be freed, sent her mind into terror. She needed to know he was all right.

Emily headed straight for the van, hearing Dearheart's footsteps behind her.

She pulled open the two heavy doors and gasped. "Jesus. No…" Charge lay there, moaning in pain. His face was so swollen, bloodied, and purple that she hardly recognized him. Blood was soaked into his white T-shirt. Fresh blood. His hands were crumpled up and shaking, close to his chest. It looked like they'd broken more than a few fingers.

She turned to Dearheart. "We had a deal." Her fists balled; her body burned with white-hot rage.

"Yes, and here he is. Take it or leave it."

"The deal was you wouldn't hurt him anymore."

"Well," Dearheart shrugged, "he didn't want

to play nice and answer our questions."

Meaning, they'd been trying to get information out of him?

She knew, with every fiber of her being, that Charge looked like this because he hadn't given in. From the looks of it, they'd stopped just shy of killing him.

All rational thought dissolved from her mind. This was the rage Flint had felt last night, only she wasn't at all interested in staying in control. "You understand that when the crew sees what you did to him, they're going to hunt you down. All of you. No easy bullets in the back of the head. No quick and painless deaths. You'll suffer just like you made him suffer." The threat came straight from her heart. She would move heaven and earth to make these people pay because, honestly, she could tolerate many things in this world. Seeing a person beaten like this, however? *No. Just…no.*

"Well," said Dearheart, "I suppose it's my lucky day, then, since I really hadn't intended on letting either of you live." His eyes flashed behind her to the rooftop of the building across the street.

It was then that she realized the van had been parked so the back doors blocked the view of anyone driving by. They blocked the view of anyone coming and going from any of the establishments in the lonely strip mall, too.

Emily frowned. "Why go through all this if you just wanted to kill us? You could have done that to begin with."

"And miss the opportunity to get the Heroin King's money back? Plus a little extra to get on his good side. All compliments of Sampson and friends. Didn't have to lift a finger."

So there it was. The piece that had been missing. And it had been so damned obvious. This was all about buying the good graces of the Heroin King—likely the Warrens' new client. According to Flint and Olivia, Dearheart probably worked for them.

Why didn't I see it before? And now, with the team out of town, there was no one to come to her aid. After she and Charge were dead, the suite forty-five members would have no one to coordinate their jobs and protect them. They'd scatter with the wind. Or maybe the Warrens planned to have Dearheart pick them off, too. Little by little. Quietly. That was what she'd do if she were trying to take over. And evil as fuck.

"Hey, but my offer still stands," Dearheart added. "If you want a job, we have plenty of opportunities for women like you."

"Like me, how?"

"You have a look about you that reminds me of a dog that's been kicked one too many times. Almost like you're expecting it. Or maybe even wanting it. Either way, I could use an obedient lapdog."

Really? Really! He was calling her a lapdog

after she came here on time—almost—with two million dollars in hand, half she'd stolen from a very dangerous man and the other half she'd scraped together in less than twenty-four hours. Sure, it had been a team effort, but the role she'd played hadn't been passive. She'd made sure they got Olivia back when everything went to hell. She'd tracked Olivia down to get the money back. "*She* is going to blow his brains out," Emily muttered bitterly to herself.

"What'd you say?"

Emily stared him in the eyes and slid out the gun Olivia had given her. She pointed it at him, fully intending to shoot, but when her finger moved to pull the trigger, she froze.

She knew why.

Everything in life came with a price. If she did this, if she killed this man, she'd be giving up a chunk of her soul when he wasn't worth the dirt on the bottom of her Lone Star State flip-flops. She was sick and tired of giving away pieces of herself to men like him.

He smiled sadistically, eyeing her gun. "I didn't come alone. You know that, yes?"

"You make a very good point." *Problem solved.* She was about to die, so screw her soul. "At least I'll go with the satisfaction of knowing you went with me, you horrible piece of—"

A gurgle from the front of the van pulled her attention away.

Olivia stepped into view, wiping a hunting knife on the leg of her jeans. "Tell your friend there, Emily, that the man posted on the roof across the street is dead. As for the guy behind the wheel, I don't think he's going anywhere other than the morgue."

"You came back?" Emily was dumbfounded.

"What are friends for?" Olivia flashed a sly smile. "Shoot him, Em. Now or never."

Emily looked down at her shaking hand, everything moving in slow motion. It was just like the other times when she'd been faced with pulling the trigger. In her head, she saw where this path would take her. But then there was the other path. Doing nothing. Walking away. And one very bad man still roaming free in the world.

Emily pulled the trigger.

CHAPTER SEVENTEEN

Emily had never slept so much in all her life. While Charge convalesced in the other room, she stayed buried beneath the covers, only popping awake to check Charge's IV, make sure he was still breathing, and to hydrate.

Olivia had helped her get in touch with the "family doctor" and given her the blue pickup truck to transport Charge from the private clinic to his cabin about three hours north of El Paso. It was the place he'd taken Emily to rest after getting her back from the cartel.

It was a quiet property, surrounded by tall pines and blue sky, perfect for recovering from three fractured ribs, a broken hand, a minor concussion, lacerations on his chest, and a very busted-up face. The doctor said it looked like they'd worked him over with a baseball bat and then a knife. He needed to rest and heal, but otherwise, he'd live.

Emily rolled out of the bed in the guest room and checked the clock on the nightstand. It was almost nine o'clock at night, and she was starving. She checked on Charge, who was still out cold. His IV was halfway done. She'd come back and change it in a bit, like the doctor showed her. A handy skill.

She went into the great room, which included the kitchen and dining area. It was the only other space besides the two bedrooms and one bath. She dug a can of chicken soup from the cupboard and poured it into a bowl to microwave.

A groan erupted from Charge's room. Emily padded to the master—a sparsely decorated space with a fireplace and a few watercolor paintings of mountains on the wood-panel walls. "You awake?"

"I gotta piss," he mumbled.

"Oh. Okay."

His left hand was all busted up, and two of his fingers on the right were broken.

Emily drew a steady breath, realizing she was going to have to help him. "I'm going to, um…I'll be right back with a—a something for you to go in."

With hot cheeks, she went to the kitchen and found a plastic pitcher. *I can't believe this.* She hadn't signed up to be a nurse. And after everything he'd done, all the lies and deceits, she really should just let him wet the bed. She'd gotten him free. She'd risked her ass to do it. *Now I have to touch his penis?* It was way too intimate.

She returned to his side and stared down at him. He looked like he was passed out again. "Charge?"

He mumbled incoherently.

"What was that?"

"Pain."

"Oh. I have some pills to give you. But first…" She flipped the quilt to the side, exposing his plain blue boxers. It surprised her that he even wore underwear. Seemed like the commando type to her.

Emily grabbed the pitcher and then looked the other way, sliding her hand into the opening of the fabric. She tried not to let her pulse skyrocket or think about what she was doing. After all, she'd been married before. She'd seen a few penises. *It's not a big dea—*

She wrapped her hand around his warm thick member. *Okay. Well, that is a big deal.*

She freed his cock and angled it toward the tilted pitcher, trying to avert her eyes as she waited.

Nothing happened.

"Emily, why is your hand on my dick?" Charge mumbled.

Emily looked up at his swollen and bruised face. "You said you need to pee."

"In the bathroom," he whispered, his voice raspy. "Help me to the bathroom. My legs are fine."

"Oh." This was embarrassing. So, so embarrassing. She slid his cock back into his shorts, vowing not to remember any details. Not the velvety texture, not the girth, and certainly not how heavy it felt in her palm. "I'm sorry. It's just that the doctor told me you might be too weak to get up for a few days, and I figured that—"

"It's fine," he mumbled. "I'm glad you're willing to go the extra mile."

"More like nine inches, but who's counting?" *Dear fuck, why did I just say that?* "Let me help you up. I'll carry your IV." The bag was set up on a small stand, but it wasn't the type with wheels.

She took his hand and helped him slowly swing his feet to the floor. "Careful," she warned as he groaned. "You have a few fractured ribs."

"I'm aware."

She hooked her arm around his and helped him to his feet. After some maneuvering of the IV, she got him to the small bathroom by letting him put his arm over her shoulders for support. Charge was a large guy—six-two or three. Solid muscular build. She was only five-five and needed to put on weight. It took all her strength to hold him steady.

She gritted her teeth, leaning into him so he could get into position. "This would have been easier if you peed when I had it ready to go."

"Your hand was cold," he muttered and started to go.

Feeling awkward, she started to ramble while averting her eyes. "Hey, if you're feeling like you can drink something, there's apple juice. I can probably take the IV out, too."

Charge didn't respond, too busy relieving himself.

After he pissed like a racehorse, she helped him back to bed and wiped down his partially bandaged hand with a soapy washcloth.

"Why are you being so nice to me?" he said, now lying down with his head propped up on a pillow.

It wouldn't be any fun to kill you in this state, so I plan to nurse you back to health first. "That's a very good question. I'm not sure."

"How did you find Ed's money?"

Charge wasn't aware of all that had gone on to come up with the two million dollars. Now one million. She'd given half to Olivia, who'd left town. It was anyone's guess if Flint was going to join her. The other million was in the hall closet, minus the ten thousand she had to pay the doctor.

"Why don't we talk about all that after you've rested up." Emily wanted to confront him. She wanted to hear why Charge had manipulated her from day one. If her assumptions were right, he had been watching her every move long before she ever met him. And all the bullshit about killing Ed? He wasn't dead. She never owed the suite forty-five crew a million dollars. Were the women Ed's group sex-trafficked really free?

"Did you tell the team I'm back?" he asked.

"Olivia said she'd post something on that florist website." Emily still had no idea how to access it.

"They have to be warned. This'll be war now." Charge winced, trying to get comfortable on the bed.

"I don't see why. We only killed three of their guys, and from what I understand, backers don't care as long as jobs are still getting done."

"Backers. Someone's been talking to you."

"It's been a very enlightening few days."

"There's more to the situation. A lot more." Charge groaned again.

Of course there was. Why would anything be simple when it came to these people? "Let me get you those pain pills and a glass of juice." She went to the kitchen area, her heart racing.

Why?

As she poured a glass and looked around the kitchen for a straw, she realized that despite her anger with Charge, she feared what came next. The moment she confronted him, he might lie again, and that was something she wouldn't tolerate. *Or maybe he's finally going to tell me the truth.* Which could possibly be worse.

Charge kept saying he believed in her, that she was strong, and she was finally beginning to believe it. She wasn't a pathetic creature like Dearheart said. She stepped up and went back to her old house. She didn't run away when Flint brought her on those jobs for the Greek or when Petri took Olivia. She didn't cower when Dearheart said he was going to kill her and Charge. She took him out.

Every step of the way, she did what she had to. And it was never for herself. She did it to protect this new, very messed-up "family" she'd stumbled into.

Only now, she wondered if it was all fake. Either way, the discussion with Charge would bring an end to their relationship. And her heart wasn't ready to let go. She had nothing. No real home, no family, no friends—none that she could contact anyway. She felt like a goddamned leaf, blowing in the ice-cold wind, which felt worse than any physical agony she'd ever known. Loneliness was the ultimate pain. On the other hand, she was learning to depend entirely on herself. That was a good thing.

Unable to find a straw, Emily returned to Charge's room with just the medicine and his juice. Charge was asleep again.

"Maybe for the best." She'd stay until he could get up on his own. It would give her time to accept what was coming. Blowing with the wind away from here.

CHAPTER EIGHTEEN

Five days later, Charge was managing to get out of bed on his own. The IV was out. He'd been eating like a horse and sleeping the rest of the time, which was why she finally had to make a run to the store a few miles away.

She pulled up to the cabin in Olivia's old pickup, spotting Charge sitting in an Adirondack chair on the front porch, showered and wearing a clean flannel and jeans. A cup of steaming coffee sat next to him on a wooden table.

It was good to see him up again. His eyes were open all the way, and he was almost recognizable.

She hopped out of the truck and grabbed the bags from the back. "You're looking like a new man," she said, stepping onto the porch.

"I feel almost human again."

"I got ham and cheese. Want a sandwich?"

"Sure."

She went inside, put the groceries away, and made his lunch. The emotion in her chest was building like a pressure cooker. Charge was going to start asking his questions again. The last few days, she'd been able to sidestep his inquiries about what had happened while he was gone, because he'd been too groggy to put up a fight. Today would be different.

I'm not ready. Whatever happened next, her heart was going to be split in two. She'd had plenty of time to think of reasons for everything he'd done, and none were good.

Basically, it all boiled down to using her—to lure Ed out of hiding, to keep her believing she was there with Charge and the team of her own free will, to get her to trust them so she'd tell them what she knew. Maybe they'd want her to do something for them when the time came.

Emily drew a shaky breath and headed outside, taking the chair on the other side of the small table on the porch. She set the sandwich next to Charge's coffee.

"Thanks," he said.

She looked straight ahead at the thick growth of pine trees running the length of the dirt road leading out. The crisp morning air filled with a palpable tension.

"Emily," Charge said, "I wanted to tell you something."

"Okay. Shoot."

"I know you don't want to talk about it, but it will help."

She looked at him. The shape of his square jaw was almost visible now that the swelling had gone down, and it was pulsing. "What do you mean?"

"It's never easy killing a person, but Dearheart isn't worth a second of guilt. The world is a better place without him."

Oh, so Charge thought her tight lips were about that. "I'm okay with it. I think," she added quietly.

"Then what's been eating at you? I can tell something's up."

She drew a slow breath, trying to form a clear thought. This conversation had to happen. But where to start?

"I just…I need…" *Oh God.*

"Whatever it is, you can tell me."

"It's not me. It's you. It's all your lies, Charge."

He stared at her for a long, silent moment. "Which ones?"

"All of 'em. Starting with why you lied about Ed being dead."

He bobbed his head slowly, unsurprised. "I meant to tell you. Eventually. But I—"

"Whatever you're about to say, don't even *think* of lying to me again. And if it makes things easier, I plan to leave no matter what you say. I've got the money to start over—money free and clear from your fabricated debts. I have no reason to stay now that you're out of bed. And, frankly, I'm tired of the games. But before I go, all I ask is that you tell the truth. I deserve that much from you."

"Yes. You do. Especially now."

"So how long were you watching me before I ran from Ed?"

Now he looked surprised. She'd figured it out. "Three months."

"Why?" she asked.

"He was a target. Him and his group."

As she guessed. "Who hired you?"

"One of the women he took was an exchange student at NYU from Colombia. Her family paid us to get her back and take care of your husband and his associates."

Ed was so stupid. He honestly believed that no one would ever come after him for taking their daughters.

"So why watch me?" she asked.

"We were watching everyone close to Ed. It's part of the vetting process."

Emily frowned. "You thought I was in on his business?"

"At first, I wasn't sure, but I realized fairly soon you were planning to run from him."

"So you *were* at the library. You followed me."

"It was various team members initially, but once they gave me their report on you, I decided to take a look for myself. I found it hard to believe you were an innocent bystander."

Well, she was. "And?"

"And then I saw him kick the crap out of you. It was about three weeks before you left him. The curtains were open in your bedroom."

Emily bit down on her lower lip. She refused to let it quiver. "How did you see—"

"The house across from you is an Airbnb," he explained.

"Oh." The shame washed over her. He'd seen what Ed did to her. She should have fought back, but at the time, she didn't know how. Things were different now. If she ever came across him again, he'd be the one cowering.

"I'm sorry he did that do you," Charge said.

"Well, not sorry enough to help me get out. You could've put a bullet in his head right then and there." That was the job, right? Charge had been hired to kill Ed.

"Yes, but Ed had more than one house running, and I couldn't do anything until we found the locations. Unfortunately, we weren't the only ones watching him. We believe someone inside the FBI was, too. He found out he was under surveillance and took off before we could move. It was just a few days after you left."

Oh my God. So had she stuck around, she probably would've been arrested. And now, the FBI probably thought she was on the run with

Ed. *Great. Wonderful.*

"So what was I to you, then?" she questioned. "Why follow me to El Paso if you knew I had nothing to do with Ed's business?"

"It's complicated." Charge exhaled, wincing and pressing his bandaged hand to his ribs.

"I'm all ears. I'd especially like to know how you got me to come work for you. Or the reason you made all this crap up about wanting me to manage your team."

She stared, waiting for an answer, but Charge wasn't speaking.

"Fine." She threw her hands in the air. "Don't tell me why you had me jump through all these hoops. Don't tell me why you blew smoke up my ass and said how much you believed in me. It doesn't matter." The frustrated tears formed in her eyes. "I mean, who does that, huh? After everything I went through? I somehow managed to pull myself from the gutter, and it was all just a joke to you." She stood up, ready to lose it. "You know what? I have no idea who you really are, but you've made a fucking idiot out of me for the last time.

"Do you understand that I risked everything to save you even though I knew you'd lied to me? Yeah, that's right. I *knew* Ed was still alive and that the job you gave me in El Paso was a setup. I *knew* you lied about your sister. I knew all of it! And I *still* saved your sorry-ass life because you saved mine." And she wasn't merely talking about the cartel thing. Charge had gotten into her head and made her see herself as something other than a victim.

If it hadn't been for that, she'd still be a prisoner—scared to death of Ed finding her, worrying about how she was going to eat or live.

Charge's square jaw ticked away, but he wouldn't look at her.

"Okay. I gave you a chance to explain yourself. Goodbye and good luck." She felt her heart crack open just a little wider. After everything, he wasn't going to tell her the truth. *To hell with him.*

She walked by him and went inside to gather the few things she had—one outfit she'd just washed, a few toiletries she'd picked up at the drugstore, and her cash.

She'd already planned it out. Olivia gave her the name of a guy in Cincinnati, some Vanderhorst dude who could set her up. Apparently, he was the king of fake identities. She'd head north, maybe to Wisconsin or North Dakota. She'd always wanted to see Wrangell, Alaska, a place her father always told her stories about when she was little. Supposedly, they had amazing sea life. From there, she'd lie low for a while and then go to Canada. Now that the FBI, Heroin King, and Warrens were looking for her, she'd have to be extremely careful.

With her bags in hand, she marched through the living room. Charge stood in the doorway, blocking it. "I fell in love with you."

Emily blinked, her heart rate going out of control. Her knees went weak. "Sorry?"

"I was watching you," he blurted out in that deep husky voice. "I saw you every day for almost a month, and one day, I found myself looking forward to it. Seeing you go for your run in the mornings. You smiling at the librarian who yelled at everyone except you. The way you held your chin up when Ed spoke down to you. I know…" He held up his bandaged right hand. "It sounds like I was being a stalker, but remember, I was paid to vet that job. You were the part of it I didn't expect."

Was this some sort of sick joke? "So you followed me to El Paso?"

"Yes. We're actually based just outside Houston, but we work in El Paso all the time. We have a few safe houses to stash weapons and supplies. That pest-control office was one of them. Hadn't used it in a while, as I'm sure you could tell."

She set her bags on the floor. None of this was making sense. And, frankly, she didn't believe him. "Why set me up with that job answering the phone? Why tell me you wanted to pull me into the group?"

"I had to have an excuse to keep you in town,

safe from *him*. The team wouldn't approve of my real motives."

The no-fraternization rule?

He added, "I needed them to trust you. I had to justify keeping you around."

"You're telling me that you…" she swallowed down a hard lump, "you love me, but then you lied about killing Ed and the money I owed and everything just to keep me around?" *Bullshit!*

"I couldn't tell the truth because you weren't one of us. So, yes, I lied about Ed and the money. I told the team to go along because it might flush him out. If you were desperate enough, you'd go looking for his money, and you might find a trail for us to pick up on too. That's what I told them."

She stared up at his horribly bruised face, trying to let it all sink in. "So many lies," she whispered.

"An unfortunate practice of the business. We tell people what they need to hear to get them to trust us. And until the team could trust you, I had to treat you like a pawn—the wife of a target on the run. It was the only way. Otherwise, the team would've figured out what was really going on."

Emily didn't know where to begin with unpacking this. She walked over to the couch and sank down, burying her face in her hands. It was all too crazy to believe.

Charge came and sat next to her. "I meant

what I said about you stepping in. I merely needed the team to see what I saw. And now they have. You kept me alive. I can step down and move on."

She dropped her hands. "So all that stuff about the cartel knowing you, that's all real? And so is this other rival group of hit men?"

He pointed to his face.

"Ah. Right."

His pale eyes filled with sincerity. "I never lied about believing in you."

"But according to you, everything else was complete emotional manipulation."

"Yes, but I do have feelings for you—it's why I told you I have a fiancée. I needed to put that distance between us. Love has no place in this profession."

She nodded, his words only sinking in so far before hitting a wall. He said he was in love with her. Was this another ploy, another lie to get her to do something?

Maybe. Maybe not. "Charge, I'm not sure if you're telling the truth, but at least I can leave here feeling less idiotic." It was far better to hear this story than the alternative: *you're nothing but a pawn. You're a fool for believing me.* Being in love with her and having to hide it from his team was a much nicer story.

He stared down at her, the two of them locking eyes, the emotion so thick she could almost pluck it from the air.

"You belong here," he said. "With us. Don't leave." His gaze drifted to her lips.

She'd kissed him a few weeks ago, after they'd first met, and it made her feel all kinds of things, but she'd quickly shut her emotions down. It didn't matter if she felt a hard physical attraction or that being near him pumped her with wild sexual thoughts. He was dangerous. And she wasn't talking about his profession. She could see herself getting lost in a man like him. Totally and utterly lost.

"I'm sorry, but even if I wanted to stay, I can't. Dearheart knew who I was, which means the Heroin King knows. I'm in the same boat as you." She paused. "Also, I can't trust you."

"I know. But that doesn't change the fact that I have your back, Emily. I always will, no matter what you think about me."

Her heart raced, fighting the urge to melt into him and his world—to forgive his lies, to accept what he was telling her now, to stay because she belonged here.

No. I can't do that to myself. She was done selling her soul for love. "Goodbye, Charge."

She stood and was almost to the door when he came after her to throw out a bomb. "Or you could stay and help me catch Ed. I think I know how to find him."

CHAPTER NINETEEN

Christ, he was good. She'd been ready to leave and never look back, but Charge knew exactly which buttons to push to suck her in again. He was the master. No doubt about it.

Standing in the doorway, she turned toward the hulking assassin standing in the great room, wearing his heart on his sleeve. Or so he wanted her to believe.

"I'm not falling for this again," she said.

"No lures. No more lies. I'll tell you anything you want, but help me find Ed."

"What for?"

He gave her a hard look.

"Don't you have enough problems as is? The cartels are on your ass, now this rival gang is after our territory, and you're a mess." She hadn't even mentioned yet that out of desperation to save his life, she'd told Olivia and Flint he was Sampson.

Who knew what the fallout would be from that?

"Add the Colombian client who's very displeased," Charge said.

And great. One more spice to season the pot. "You didn't find his daughter?"

Charge shook his head no. "Ed took off before we could make him tell us what happened to her."

"What about his brother and the rest of the men?"

"Wherever they went, they planned well. The only traces we found were their abandoned cars parked at a few airports, Miami harbor, and even one in El Paso. They were ready to disappear."

"Ed said as much in his letter," she muttered.

"What letter?"

"I found it at my house in Ed's office. It said I needed to run and stay running. Oh, and he left me a hundred thousand cash. A very generous consolation for all the torment," she said sarcastically. "But it was a relief knowing he never put a hit on me."

Charge looked away. "I'm sorry. I knew who you were and needed to give you a reason for it." Charge had known her real name and that she'd been Ed's wife. Charge's excuse had been that Ed put a hit out on her. Not true.

She bobbed her head. "You could have saved yourself a lot of trouble if you'd just told me everything."

His dark brows furrowed and his jaw tightened.

"Sorry." She raised her hands in surrender. "I forgot; you're not in the trust business."

"Not with outsiders, but you're far from that now. You know enough to put me in a bad spot with my team."

She stared in confusion.

Charge continued, "If they knew how I feel about you, they wouldn't be happy. The rules are strongly enforced, and what I did to keep you close would be treason in their minds."

She thought of Flint and Olivia. "What's the punishment for breaking the rules?"

"No, Emily. I meant what I said. I would never cross that line, no matter how much I—"

"I didn't mean anything by it, okay? It was just a question."

He stared for a second, those pale gray eyes riddled with emotion.

"I'm not…in love with you," she added truthfully. Physical attraction wasn't love. "In fact, you scare the hell out of me, Charge."

"I scare you?"

"More than Ed ever did."

He went over to the couch and took a seat again, leaning back to likely relieve the pressure on his ribs.

She shut the front door and went to sit next to him. "Just being honest."

"Those are words I never hoped to hear from

a woman, let alone you. I would never harm you."

That wasn't true. "I think we can both agree that the worst kinds of wounds aren't the ones that need Band-Aids or stitches."

"I'm not sure that makes me feel better."

Too bad. She wasn't here to make him feel good about the games and lies. She still wasn't sure he was being honest about being in love with her. "Can you tell me something?"

He gave her a nod.

Even now, all dented and banged up, sitting next to him gave her a small rush. Something about Charge was exciting. Physically and emotionally. He wasn't hard on the eyes either. Thick black hair. Intense eyes. Nice lips. He was classic handsome and tough. *And never gonna happen.*

"Say I help you find Ed. What next? Because I know you'll just be dangling another carrot to get me to stay."

"Why do you think that?"

She flashed a frown at him.

"Fine. I would tell you that our plan to have you lead, and for me to step back and be purely operational, was still valid. I would tell you that you could do a lot more good in this world being Sampson than you ever could running off to hide with a bunch of cartel money."

The cash she had was actually a mishmash of Ed's money, the Greek's money, and Petri's money. Olivia had taken off with the cartel cash. She said she could clean it—no problem—so Emily was better off with the non-drug money.

"And then what?" Emily asked. "Where would it end? Where would my life go if I said yes to working with you and suite forty-five?"

"I won't lie. It's dangerous work. Eventually you burn out or you're forced out because your cover's blown. You'd have to find a new Sampson and retire."

"How long?" she asked.

"Why do you ask?"

Because she needed to understand what lie ahead if she stayed. Would there be an out? Or did it always have a tragic ending? "I want to know if the Sampson retirement plan is at the bottom of a lake in a steel drum, or if there's a real way out."

"It could end with you stepping down after getting the beating of a lifetime." He referred to his little vacation with Dearheart.

Fun. "What did he want from you anyway?"

"Everything. Anything. Clients' names, bank accounts, operator information. He wanted anything he could use as leverage."

"What did you tell him?"

Charge cleared his throat, looking uncomfortable.

"You said you'd tell me everything," she pushed.

"Each of us memorizes what we call 'the movie.' It's a detailed story that comes complete with real bank account information, names of fake clients and operators, addresses of safe houses, and other details. Everything is real—every name, every account, every location. But it's all fake."

"I don't understand."

"The names in our movie belong to people who fit the part but have nothing to do with us. They're real-life people who, if they happened to be caught and tortured to death, probably deserve it, but can't give up real information. The bank accounts have real money in them. The safe houses are places we keep as movie sets. Like that pest-control office you first went to. They're unoccupied properties we use as we see fit. The movie has enough information to keep people like Dearheart or the Warrens occupied for weeks before they realize they've been fed a bunch of dead ends."

"Why do that when they'll eventually find out and just beat the truth out of you?"

"It's not meant for the person who's being interrogated."

Emily chewed on his comment. "It gives the team time to realize something's up, so they can move or warn people or whatever."

"Yes."

"So you gave Dearheart a rundown of your movie, and he bought it?"

"Yes. Though, he would've eventually figured it out."

"And why do the Warrens want to take over the border again?"

"The Colombian client, the one whose daughter was taken, controls this side of the border. Heroin King hired the Warrens to get rid of us so we'd stop protecting the Colombian client."

Whoa. Whoa. Whoa. "You mean the woman Ed took is really your client's daughter?"

Charge nodded.

"And you're protecting a Colombian drug lord?"

"Not exactly. Our backers protect him, and their interests are our interests. You have to let go of idealism when dealing with that world. The devils own it. They run it. If we're lucky, we get to choose the lesser of hells, which is the group that wreaks less havoc on the communities."

"That's not right." It was insanity, actually.

"No, it's not, but what other choice is there? Let the Heroin King take over? His cartel doesn't care who they kill. They'll gladly turn the border into their private war zone. The Colombian wants a quiet, steady income and targets recreational users. That's far better than seeing children mowed down in the street while the northern cartels fight for territory. With the Colombian in charge, things stay quiet. We make sure any attempts by the Mexican cartels to change that are stopped."

"I can't believe this." She'd thought they were the good guys.

"It's ugly, Emily, but it's either the Colombian and his coke, or it's heroin pouring in. Which do you think is the lesser of two evils?"

"Those are the choices?" It was awful. Just awful.

"Until people on this side of the border stop asking for this shit, then yes. Those are the choices."

"So just accept it?" she asked contemptuously.

"I don't accept anything. I support whichever option results in fewer bodies—children, mothers, sons, daughters. A life saved is a life saved."

She knew he'd served in the military. She guessed his philosophy about "lesser evils" came from that—being taught to assess options in terms of casualties. It was pragmatic and realistic, not idealistic.

But for her there was right. And there was wrong.

He was basically saying that suite forty-five was a perpetual Band-Aid to prevent a bad situation from getting worse. Unfortunately, given the competing factions on the border, she didn't know if there was an alternative. But there had to be one. Right? A way to shut all the drug dealers down for good?

So," Charge pushed, "what other questions do

you have?"

"Too many to count."

"Start with the most important."

"Why did you say you love me?"

"Mmm… you really are a born killer. Go straight for the jugular."

"That's not funny." She got up and went to the cabinet, grabbing a glass. She poured herself a whisky from one of the bottles he had stashed in the cupboard. None for him. He was still on meds.

"A little early for that?" he said.

"Never too early when you're preventing a nervous breakdown." She took a swig and set the glass on the kitchen counter. "Answer me."

"Why do I…?"

"Yeah. Love me. Why's that so hard for you to say all of a sudden? Unless it's just another lie."

He drew a slow breath. "I honestly don't know. Maybe it's the way you look at me—like I'm not a monster for what I do. Maybe it's because I see you're not a dog who's been kicked one too many times."

"So you heard that."

"Yes. And it proved what a stupid asshole he was. Never say that to a woman—unarmed or otherwise. She'll gut you with her teeth and fingernails if she has to. Next question?"

"What happens—really happens—if the team finds out?"

"About what?" he asked.

She wanted to say "us," but there was no us. There was just him and his feelings. She didn't want anything from him other than honesty. "That you lied about your reasons for keeping me around."

"They won't find out unless you tell them. Do you plan to tell them, Emily?"

"No."

"Then what more is there to settle? I need you to help me hunt down Ed. I promise to be truthful with you going forward. You'll take over the team while I fade into the background. Sounds fairly simple to me." He got up, went to his room, and lay down on his bed.

How the hell could he think this conversation was done?

She marched in after him. "Hey, I didn't agree to anything. I was talking hypotheticals. And I'm in no better position than you to run suite forty-five, remember?" She pointed to her face. "The cartels know who I am."

"They don't think you're running things. They won't suspect you're Sampson. They think you're a low-level gatekeeper."

There was that word again. "What's a gate-keeper?"

"It's a person who runs messages to the boss. You know how to set up a meeting with Sampson too, but you don't know enough to tell anyone where he is if they catch you."

"Always with the answers." She scowled.

"What more do you want to know? Just say it. Because I'm tired. I'm in pain. And I need to rest so I can help the other thirty-eight operators avoid whatever the fuck is coming."

Thirty-six. Olivia had already left. Possibly Flint had too.

"So are you in or out, Emily?"

"I need a few days to think. More sleep would be good. Also, I wouldn't mind closing my eyes, knowing I was going to wake up alive." Besides regular meals, that was the other luxury she missed most.

He stared at her face for a long moment. "Then come here." He glanced at the spot next to him on the large bed.

She knew she shouldn't. She knew it would only make it harder to keep a clear head around him, but she needed the comfort more than she needed to behave rationally at the moment. The last weeks and months were taking a toll on her in every way possible. She couldn't remember the last time anyone held her.

She walked around the bed and slid under the covers next to Charge's warm body. She put her cheek on his chest, making him flinch. "Sorry. Forgot about the stitches."

"It's fine." He pulled her closer, into the heat of him. And for the first time in a long time, she closed her eyes, feeling like she wasn't alone. But being close to a deadly hit man who claimed to love her, who would kill for her, was a bad idea. He could break her. For good this time. The like she felt could easily turn into something more.

"Just because I'm sleeping next to you doesn't mean I've agreed to stay," she said.

"And just because you grabbed my cock doesn't mean I expect you to."

She smiled. This was just what she needed right now. Probably him, too. A chance to heal.

Before the next battle.

THE PAUSE

WANT AN ALERT FOR THE NEXT BOOK?

OPTION #1: Hope that M.O.'s carrier pigeon lands on your windowsill with a new release tied to its neck.
Success Rate: -10%

OPTION #2: Stalk M.O. on Facebook and hope the FB spy-bots bless you with an announcement mixed in with all those other ads about bras, face cream, and meal kits.
Success Rate: 5%

OPTION #3: Stalk M.O. on Instagram and hope M.O.'s incredibly entertaining posts float to the top of your feed.
Success Rate: 20%

OPTION #4: Sign up for M.O.'s release alerts and perhaps learn the author's true identity. (Ha! So hard, right?) But most definitely, you will hear about new books before everyone else.
Success Rate: 100% (Okay. It's really like 99% but whatever. It's the best chance you've got! And M.O. is way too busy writing to spam you, so there's that.)

SIGN UP HERE

www.authormomack.com

Still haven't read Book 1? Check out this excerpt
of *SHE'S GOT THE GUNS*

★ ★ ★

CHAPTER ONE

Emily Rockford sat anxiously behind the beat-up
reception desk, with nothing to keep her company
aside from the faded yellow wallpaper and the
monotonous grinding sound of the AC unit. A
unit that was crammed into a partially boarded-up
window, had no off switch, and dribbled rust-
brown sludge down the wall. She was pretty sure
the grungy brown carpet underneath it was rotten,
but what did that matter?

This office is a shithole, she thought. *And why
would anyone hardwire the AC to run nonstop?*
Granted, they were in Texas and, like today, the
weather could get unbearably hot. But no off

switch? No way to unplug it?

Very strange, she thought.

Then again, nothing about this situation felt right. Not the terms of her employment, not this abandoned, run-down strip mall, and certainly not the fact there was no business name posted anywhere. The only thing identifying this office was the "Suite #45" painted outside in chunky black letters above the frosted-glass door.

What the hell were they *really* selling here? Mr. Sampson, the man who'd hired her, said they performed "discreet pest control" for the sort of people who didn't want their neighbors knowing they had roach issues. "It's a status thing," he'd said.

But this was El Paso, Texas, not Beverly Hills. People were more caught up with everyday life than what their neighbors thought. It was why she'd moved here. Lack of *noseys*.

Emily hugged her pilling white cardigan to her shivering body. Any second now, she would have to bust open the AC's front panel and shut off that icebox. The only reason she hadn't yet was out of respect for Mr. Sampson, who didn't vibe as friendly. At least not over the phone. She hadn't actually met the guy, despite three days passing since she'd started work. "Work" being a term she used loosely here. All she did was sit and wait for the phone to ring.

It never did.

Then, at the end of each shift, she found one hundred dollars deposited into her Zelle account, just as they'd agreed over the phone.

Well, the man did say he might be late coming in to train me. Only, she'd thought he meant hours, not days.

Emily got up from her creaky chair, one of those antique oak things with metal wheels and ass-shaped grooves carved into the seat. With body heat on her mind, she started walking circles around the small, nearly empty office that contained three beige filing cabinets against the back wall, her prison-gray desk made of sheet metal (nothing in the drawers), and a grimy Mr. Coffee. The thing had at least an inch of scale caked inside the carafe. *Nasty.*

She glanced at the machine, noting a giant cockroach skittering across the yellow Formica counter off to the side of the room. It stopped, turned in her direction as if warning her off, and then disappeared down the rust-stained sink at the end.

She lifted a brow. *Pest control, huh?* Well, if that was really Mr. Sampson's business, he sucked at it. The lack of customers was a huge hint, too.

With the blood now flowing again, Emily walked back to the desk and checked her cell for the fiftieth time. Still no new emails from Sampson.

This is insane. Where was he? Why hire her to

just sit around and do nothing? She replayed their one and only phone conversation in her mind: "The key to the front door will be taped under the doormat. Keep it safe with you at all times. You are to answer the phone and take messages. No questions. Ever. No conversations. Ever. Just take the message, hang up. If I'm not in the office, place the message in the top drawer of the desk. That's it."

"I think I can handle that," she'd said, knowing full well the entire situation was shady as fuck. But she had to pay rent. She had to eat. The challenge was, employment options were limited for people like her—no real skills, no references, no college education. Ed had never allowed her to work or take classes. Moving to El Paso was supposed to be the first step to a fresh start. Unfortunately, after two weeks she'd already burned through the small amount of cash she'd managed to scrape together before running.

New identities cost a lot.

The red push-button phone on her desk began blaring with a high-pitched ring, making her jump in her black flats.

"Sonofa…" She pressed her palm over her heart. She'd never actually heard the damned thing make a noise until now. Not a soul had passed through the door either.

She reached for the handpiece, not knowing what to expect. "He-hello?"

"Tell Sampson," said a cold, gravelly voice, "customer ninety-two's rat has been taken care of."

His voice sent a chill down her spine. *I bet he killed the poor critter just by talking to it.* She grabbed the pad of legal paper on her desk and wrote down the message. Should she tell the caller that Mr. Sampson was MIA?

No. She shouldn't get involved. She was there to take messages from ten a.m. to four p.m. Monday through Friday. That was it. The less she knew about whatever this place really was, the better.

"Got it," she said, "and may I say who's call-ing?"

There was a long, static-filled pause. "Who the fuck is this?"

Shit. She wasn't supposed to ask questions. "My name is…*Jane*. I just started working here." She wasn't about to give him her name, even if Emily Rockford was an alias. She didn't have another two grand to buy another identity that came with a social security card and an Illinois driver's license of a twenty-six-year-old woman who vaguely resembled her: five-five height, Caucasian, green eyes, brown hair, and one hundred and thirty pounds.

"Well, *Jane*," the man said in a bone-chilling voice, "I suggest you shut your fucking mouth and pass along the message." The line went dead.

Emily hung up and released a slow breath. She had a very bad feeling about this job. Very bad. But until she found something else, this was better than sleeping in the gutter. Or worse, next to Ed.

CHAPTER TWO

Wearing her only set of PJs—a lame yellow duckie T-shirt combo with matching shorts that she'd found in the 99-cent bin at Goodwill— Emily spent the long muggy night tossing and turning with wave after wave of internal debate.

That voice in her sour stomach screamed not to go back to that office in the morning. Unfortunately, her stomach kept being overruled by necessity, including the need to find a less dumpy apartment. It was bad enough that used needles littered the walkway just outside her door each morning, but she couldn't even get a decent night's sleep. The couple next door spent most nights drinking and fighting. Their cruel words— *"You're nothing. You're a stupid whore. I should kill you!"*—reminded her of the existence she'd left behind. Except, in the here and now, the yelling made her anxious. Back home, the yelling had given her a sick kind of relief.

Emily rolled to her side. It was painful to look back and know it had taken almost three years to grow a pair and leave Ed, but there hadn't been a day when she didn't think about running. Some days were better than others, like the days when Ed came home from work and spewed the most vile, hateful things. Those were the good days. Yelling didn't leave bruises. It was when Ed turned silent that she had to worry. Those were the bad days.

Never again. She rolled to her other side, the phantom ache of a once cracked rib throbbing against the mattress. *Put it out of your mind. You're free now.* She stared at the orange-and-black striped pattern on her window, a product of blinds that didn't close properly and the street-lamps just outside.

I really have to find a better place. But that wasn't a priority. She needed to save every dime she could. It was June, and the fall semester at the junior college would be starting in September. She planned to get her certificate in one impossible backbreaking semester and then get a job as a bookkeeper. A safe home with respectable employment was all she needed.

Patience and hard work. I can get there. Besides, no turning back now. Ed would kill her if he tracked her down. This path, as difficult as it might be, was the only way.

By nine a.m. the next morning, she'd gone for a three-mile run, showered, and dressed in one of the three outfits she'd purchased from the thrift store. Solid-color blouses and black skirts. Modest, unnoticeable. She'd even dyed her red hair to a chestnut brown. Emily Rockford was someone you'd look at and not really see. Utterly forgettable.

The old, pathetic her had worn flowery dresses and strappy leather sandals. The old her was expected to look cute to please Ed, especially when his friends came over to play poker. *Total assholes.* They would wait until Ed was too drunk to notice anything but the cards in his hands, and corner her in the kitchen. They'd grab her ass and breasts. The one time she'd tried to tell Ed about how they treated her, she got blamed and ended up with a black eye.

"Stop acting like a slut, and they'll stop treating you like one," he'd said.

Never again. Never again would she dress up if she didn't want to. Never again would she allow a person's hands on her like that.

Now wearing a navy blue blouse and a black skirt, with her unremarkable brown hair in a ponytail, Emily caught the bus for work and ended up arriving a few minutes early, so she ran across the street to the gas station. There was no bathroom in the office that she saw, and if there was one somewhere in the vacant strip mall, she doubted she'd want to use it.

She purchased a bottle of water and a small bag of pretzels, the cheapest things she could find, and hugged them to her chest as she jogged back, weaving through the logjam of cars stopped at the light.

Panting, she stepped up on the sidewalk and noticed a man—tall, lanky, dark hair—standing just outside the suite. He wore brown pants, a white shirt, and black dress shoes. *The outfit of a person who doesn't want to draw attention.* Just like her.

Could that be Mr. Sampson? But he looked too young, maybe thirtyish. Mr. Sampson had the gruff voice of a much older man.

Emily cautiously approached, noting the guy's sweaty face and shifty dark eyes. "Hi. Are you waiting for…" *No questions. No questions.* "I'm Jane, the receptionist." She held out her free hand.

He nodded but didn't take it. "I was told to come here and leave my message." He gave her his back, waiting for her to unlock the door.

Okay… Who showed up at an office to "leave a message"? Why not call? Why not text or email Mr. Sampson?

"Mind hurrying? I got things to do," the man urged.

Now it was her turn to have shifty eyes. Was anyone else around to hear her scream if this guy pulled something?

There wasn't.

All she had was the passing cars behind her, made up of people on their way south of the border to work at one of the factories, most of them distracted by their phones and traffic. Besides, who could hear anything over the constant roar of semis going north, carrying goods out of Mexico?

"One sec. Let me get the key." She slid her hand into her oversized black purse, making sure she'd brought her pepper spray. It was right where she wanted it, in that little pocket meant for her cell. "Here it is." She produced the key and opened the front door. The man followed her in.

"Why's it so cold?" he asked.

She headed straight to her desk, avoiding eye contact. Whoever this man was, whatever business he had with Mr. Sampson, it felt safer not to remember his face.

"Um, yeah. I think the AC's busted. Won't shut off." She set down her items from the gas station but kept her purse slung on her shoulder for easy reaching.

"Guess it's better than the alternative: no AC at all. Looks like it's going to be a scorcher today."

They were getting perilously close to having a conversation—against Mr. Sampson's rules.

She nodded and grabbed her pencil, making sure to put the desk between her and the man.

"Ready."

He slid an envelope from his back pocket and set it on the desk.

This was his message?

Now she *had* to look at him. He seemed to expect her to say or do something with it. But what? "Um. Thank you. I'll put this here." *I don't see you. I will not remember the scar on your upper lip or the color of your dark eyes.* She opened the top drawer and deposited the envelope. "I'll be sure your message is given to Mr. Sampson."

He narrowed his eyes. "That's it? I hand you fifty thousand to take care of my pest problem, and we're done?"

Fifty thousand? That was a lot of money just to kill a rat or take care of some roaches. Now she had zero doubt that Mr. Sampson *was* in the extermination business—the human kind.

Hell, maybe she'd known it the moment she walked in here, but before this, there was a plausible deniability angle. And she'd been hungry. After today, she couldn't look the other way, and she wasn't about to get caught up with someone even shadier than Ed. *I need to get the hell out of here.*

"I'm sorry. I'm just the receptionist. I take messages. Nothing more." Emily forced a polite smile to her lips, wanting the man to leave so she could quickly do the same.

"So when's Sampson coming, then?"

A very good question. "I just take messages," she repeated. *No conversations. No questions. Please go.*

"Fine. Tell him to call Rick ASAP." He pressed the tip of his index finger to the top of the desk. "And this job had better be done by Saturday like he promised."

It was Thursday. She had no clue if the job would get done or if she could deliver the message. Basically, she couldn't promise him anything.

Her stomach knotted into a nauseating lump. There was a part of her—a big, sick, damaged part—that didn't want to displease this guy. Ed had beaten the fear of men into her. It ran cold through her veins like a nightmare spiked with broken glass. It smelled of stale urine, from when she'd pissed herself after being tied up in a closet for two days.

She blinked up at Rick, willing the pleasant smile to stay put. "Of course. I'll give him the message."

Rick stared for a long moment, his right eye twitching, before he finally turned and left.

"Jesus." She tilted her head back toward the water-stained ceiling. Yesterday, this place felt like rock bottom, but little had she known there was a trapdoor beneath her feet, waiting to take her lower. It was time to go.

She eyed the drawer. *Fifty thousand. Fifty thousand dollars.* If she worked five days a week for the next year, the most she could pull in was twenty-six thousand. She knew because she'd been obsessing over money. How much could she make? Was it enough to pay rent and tuition? Screw grocery shopping. She could go to the food bank or hit the dollar store once a day. A person could live off of peanut butter crackers, baked beans, Vienna sausages, ramen, and that fake orange drink crap with vitamin C. Sure, she'd die of a heart attack at forty years old, but forty was better than twenty-five—her current age.

"Forty." She chuckled bitterly and shoved her water and pretzels into her oversized purse. "At this rate, I'll be lucky to make it to thirty." Ed would never stop looking. He wouldn't rest until she was dismembered, the pieces placed in ten different suitcases and sprinkled across one hundred and thirty miles of New Jersey coastline. Add to that threat her uncanny ability to pick the most dangerous people to connect herself with and an early death was a sure thing.

She headed for the front door and was about to reach for the handle when the door jerked open. Startled, Emily gasped and looked up, locking eyes with the tall man blocking her path. He looked to be in his early thirties. He had tanned skin, unkempt black hair, and a sturdy build. His clothes—faded jeans, heavy military-style boots, and a black T-shirt that hugged his broad chest—said he was the type who *wanted* to be noticed, that he'd fuck you up if you messed with him. His soulless gray eyes said he wouldn't give a shit if you cried about it when he did.

"Where the hell is my money?" he said with a scratchy, deep voice.

It was him, the man who'd called yesterday and told her to shut the fuck up.

She didn't like being spoken to that way, but out of self-preservation, Emily pushed the anger down a deep dark hole inside her mind where she kept all the bad stuff. It was getting pretty crowded in there.

"I'm sorry. I'm just the receptionist. I answer the phone. I take messages. That's it," she said, praying that he too would just leave. There'd be no hope if he wanted to hurt her, which she assumed he would if he didn't get his way. She knew the type. *Dangerous.*

He narrowed those gray eyes. "Get Sampson on the phone."

"I'm sorry," she repeated, her voice as level as she could make it, "I just take messages."

"You're fucking telling me you can't call him?"

She shook her head no.

He stepped forward, forcing her back against the desk, the front door closing behind him. He leaned down so she had a clear view of the displeasure in his eyes. "He knows the rules. He knows the consequences. If I leave here without my money, I'll be forced to put a bullet in someone's head. And, just in case you're wondering, I only plan to stay for sixty seconds." He reached one arm behind him.

She guessed he had a gun back there. *Dangerous. Why did I have to be right about him?* Maybe it was one of the few perks of her past life—she could now spot an Ed from a mile away.

"I want. My fifty. Thousand," he added.

Fifty. Fifty. Her hands shaking, she slipped around to the other side of the desk and yanked open the drawer. "Here. Take it." She slid the envelope toward him.

He snagged it, looked inside, and offered a snarl. "Tell Sampson to call me. Next time I have to come looking for my money, I'll be going to his home, not his office."

She watched the man leave, noting the huge gun shoved in the waistband of his jeans at the small of his back.

I'm so done here. Whatever this place was, whatever services they provided, she was not having any of it.

She waited a minute, to ensure the guy was gone, and then walked outside, locked the door, and threw the key under the mat. Tomorrow she would start combing the job ads, but she was never coming back to this place.

FOR MORE, GO TO:

authormomack.com/shesgottheguns

ABOUT THE AUTHOR

Obviously, M.O. Mack is a cover name. Don't bother looking for the author's true identity. She must remain secret due to the sensitive information written in her stories… Okay, most of all that is total rubbish! M.O. is a full-time author from the great state of Arizona, who loves making stuff up and hates a slow story. The faster the better!

Most days, M.O. tries to avoid the news (too violent) so it doesn't interfere with writing funny, but quasi-violent stories.

Stalk M.O! Or, better yet, sign up for new release alerts!
RELEASE ALERTS:
authormomack.com/meet-m-o-mack
Facebook: facebook.com/AuthorMOMack
Instagram: instagram.com/author_mo_mack
Amazon: amazon.com/author/momack
Goodreads:
goodreads.com/author/show/20495694.M_O_Mack
Pinterest: pinterest.com/Author_MO_Mack

www.ingramcontent.com/pod-product-compliance
Lightning Source LLC
Chambersburg PA
CBHW061246120726

48001CB00001B/165